The Mouth Mechanic

Mike Paull

The Mouth Mechanic

I stepped into my private office, and in an instant, my feeling of omnipotence disappeared as my sympathetic nervous system began pouring adrenalin into my arteries. My desk drawers had been ripped from their slots and thrown against the walls. My papers were strewn all over the floor, and my desk computer had been smashed with a paperweight that was still lodged in its screen. What most unnerved me, though, was the Kryptonite that hung from the corner ceiling—a hangman's rope with my business card wedged into its knot.

What They Are Saying About *The Mouth Mechanic*

"Filled with intrigue, suspense and many laugh-out-loud moments, Mike Paull's *The Mouth Mechanic* is a taut, well-constructed page-turner that has a personality of its own and is terrifically entertaining. For mystery lovers and anyone who enjoys a gripping, fun read that'll keep you guessing until nearly the end, it will not disappoint."
—Lynn Solte, author, *In the Blink of an Eye*
Hollywood, FL

"I raced through this gripping book, cheering for Rick Rose, forensic odontologist", as he navigates his first case. A loveable, self-deprecating, and witty protagonist, he hooked me from the first page. I'll definitely be back for more.
—Andrea Barton, author, *The Godfather of Dance,* Melbourne, Australia

"Spending reading time with Rick Rose, odontologist extraordinaire of Mike Paull's *The Mouth Mechanic*, rewards with a fast-paced, perplexing tale of mystery and unchartered espionage. Rick's encounters with danger are laced with hilarious wit, humbleness, and doubts as he uncovers a nefarious plot for world rule. Entertaining, well-written, and I highly recommend it!
—Karen Hudgins, author, *Night of the Scarab,*
Colorado Springs, CO

The Mouth Mechanic

Mike Paull

A Wings ePress, Inc.
Forensic Crime Novel

Wings ePress, Inc.

Edited by: Jeanne Smith
Copy Edited by: Christie Kraemer
Executive Editor: Jeanne Smith
Cover Artist: Trisha FitzGerald-Jung
Image from Pixabay

All rights reserved

Names, characters and incidents depicted in this book are products of the author's imagination or are used fictitiously. Any resemblance to actual events, locales, organizations, or persons, living or dead, is entirely coincidental and beyond the intent of the author or the publisher.

No part of this book may be reproduced or transmitted in any form or by any means, electronic or mechanical, including photocopying, recording, or by any information storage and retrieval system, without permission in writing from the publisher.

Wings ePress Books
www.wingsepress.com

Copyright © 2024 by: Mike Paull
ISBN 979-8-89197-991-8

Published In the United States Of America

Wings ePress, Inc.
3000 N. Rock Road
Newton, KS 67114

Dedication

To Hank and Irene & Julian and Sylvia.
Gone, but never forgotten.

"Life always offers you a second chance,
it's called tomorrow."
---Dylan Thomas

One

If it's true that good luck is the result of good planning, then it stands to reason that dumb luck is the result of not planning at all. I never planned to end up where I did. Call it fate or destiny or even karma, but the confluence of pushy parents, an addiction to alcohol and the State of California Professional Code created the perfect storm that led me to a dissection table in the basement of the San Francisco morgue.

I was raised in Brooklyn, New York, where if you were Jewish, and not named Neil Diamond or Jerry Seinfeld, your parents pushed you hard to become a doctor. I did some quick calculation of the number of years it would take and decided the idea didn't appeal to me. Instead, I negotiated with my dad and, after hours of haggling, we agreed I would go for a dental degree. It was close enough for him; dentists wore white coats and people called them doctor. It wasn't until four years later, after I was accepted to UCLA dental school, that my father realized it was going to cost him two hundred and fifty thousand dollars. All of a sudden, he began to picture me as a successful plumber or electrician, but it was too late. In July, 2008, I packed my bags and headed for Los Angeles.

Coming from the New York area, I never felt comfortable in L.A. Maybe it was the absence of snow in the winter or the smog in the summer or maybe it was all the plastic surgery survivors who roamed the streets, but after graduation I couldn't wait to get out of there. I moved north and opened a practice in Marin County, an upscale community just across the Golden Gate Bridge from San Francisco. When I had the sign made for my new office, the shingle was too small to fit my name, so I changed it— my name, that is. I went from Richard Rosenkofsky to Rick Rose. It was a twofer; it fit perfectly on the sign and for the first time in my life people would be able to pronounce it.

One of my first patients was a beautiful young woman named Joselle Freeman. It was a bonus that she too was Jewish. It gave my mother one less thing to criticize when I married Josie a year later. We never had any kids. Either I was firing blanks or she wasn't an egg producer, but whichever, it caused problems with our relationship. It didn't bother me that much, but it took a toll on Josie. Five years later, her grandmother died and left her a good deal of money. She bought a condo in nearby Tiburon, packed up her clothes, took custody of the cat and left me alone in our thirty-five hundred square foot home.

I wasn't a happy camper and without realizing it, I slowly revised my drinking habits. I was used to having a beer or two before dinner, but over time I graduated to martinis. I also changed my drinking schedule. My six o'clock starting time moved up to five and not long after that moved to noon when I would sneak in an old-fashioned or a Manhattan at lunchtime.

When I began keeping a flask in my desk drawer, the fall came swiftly. One of my assistants smelled alcohol on my breath at ten in the morning and reported me to the state dental board. They suspended my license and put me into what they called a diversion program—kind of an AA for people who wear white coats and latex gloves.

The program did in fact divert me—right out of practice. By the time the board returned my license, all my patients had disappeared. I broke my lease, sold my equipment, and pondered what I was going to do with a dental license and nowhere to use it.

A buddy of mine offered me an apartment in a building he owned in the upscale Pacific Heights neighborhood of the city. I jumped at it. I sold my house, moved to San Francisco and began living off the equity while I tried to figure out how to put my life back together. After two months of frustration, I was sorting through the junk mail when I spotted a professional flyer from the City and County of San Francisco. They were looking for a *forensic odontologist*. I had only a vague idea of what that was, but the ad stated a dental license was required, and the starting salary was $136,400. How bad could it be?

I googled the job title and found forensic odontologists were dentists who helped in criminal investigations, especially in cases where nobody could identify who the dead guy was. I filled out an application along with my curriculum vitae—a fancy name for a resumé—which I beefed up with my short list of accomplishments. I thought it best to leave off my 2019 graduation from the alcohol diversion program.

Apparently, the offbeat idea of working on dead patients didn't appeal to many dentists. I'm pretty sure I was the only applicant. The county paid for a three-month course, after which

I was given a diploma with the word *certified* written in twenty-eight-point Segoe Script outlined in genuine artificial gold leaf. I was ready for my first case, or so I thought.

~ * ~

The HR department assigned me to Dr. Alexandra Keller, the chief medical examiner for San Francisco. I expected to meet a woman with gray hair tied in a bun, who wore wire framed glasses hanging from a chain. My stereotypical thinking was a hundred and eighty degrees off point. Dr. Keller had to be the most gorgeous pathologist in the country. I figured she was about forty, maybe five years older than I, but she certainly didn't look it. She was blessed with shining red hair, bright green eyes, and the warmest smile I'd ever seen. She thrust out her palm and said, "Dr. Rose, I'm Alex, can I call you Rick?"

I hadn't blushed in twenty years, but I felt I was doing so then. "Oh, sure... uh, Alex." I shook her hand and hoped she didn't notice the sweat.

When she took back her hand, I was relieved to see she didn't wipe it on her slacks. "I've been looking forward to your arrival," she said. "You come with great credentials."

I wondered if she had me mixed up with some other dentist, like maybe William Morton, the guy who discovered the use of ether as a general anesthetic. It must have been the flattery that caused me to say, "I'm ready to jump right in."

Dr. Keller—Alex—handed me a thick folder. It was filled with photos, the kind that put my stomach into a tug of war with itself while it decided whether breakfast should stay in place or not. The full-face shots looked male, but I wasn't sure. The cheeks were swollen and covered with blood and the lips were torn open, exposing a couple front teeth. I flipped to the torso shots and my suspicion was confirmed. The deceased was, in fact, a man.

Alex must have read my expression. She asked if I'd like a water or a juice or something else to drink. What I really wanted were a couple Pepto-Bismols, but I said, "Sure, water would be nice."

An assistant brought in a bottle of club soda. I took it and sat in front of Alex's desk. From my vantage point, I had an unobstructed view of a human skeleton mounted on a stand and a wall-size technicolored poster of the body's major organs.

"You came on board at just the right time," Alex said.

"Really. How so?"

"Those photos are of a John Doe. He had no identification, and his prints weren't on any local, state or federal registry."

I knew he didn't check into the morgue on his own, so I asked, "Where did they find him?"

"The day before yesterday was garbage day in North Beach. When a garbage dumpster behind The Stinking Rose restaurant was emptied at six in the morning, John Doe came rolling out dressed in full formal wear—a black tux, a bowtie and a silk cummerbund."

"Huh, remind me never to eat there again."

Alex stood and made a move toward the door. "Are you ready to meet him in person?"

I suddenly realized that maybe I wasn't ready for this job, and I was pretty sure I wasn't ready to be introduced to a corpse, so I stood my ground like a puppy who refuses to go outside when he has to pee.

Alex cocked her head. "Rick, are you coming?"

My mom used to say, "in for a penny, in for a pound." I nodded as if I knew what I was doing, but down deep my gut told me I was going to have to wing it. I pasted on a smile and said, "Yeah, sure, I'm coming."

Two

The morgue was in the basement, two flights below the offices. I was up for taking the elevator, but Alex said she needed the exercise. She looked pretty fit to me, and she was the boss, so I followed her down the stairway. "We're meeting Jim Allen in the morgue," she said. "He's the detective assigned to this case."

The temperature dropped in a straight line with the elevation and by the time we reached the basement, it was downright cold. I had on a pair of khakis, a polo and a blazer, but I was shivering. Down the hall, I could see a good-looking guy in a leather jacket standing in front of the morgue. He broke into a big smile when he saw us. I assumed it wasn't for me.

When we approached, the man leaned forward and gave Dr. Keller a peck on the cheek. Alex didn't respond other than making introductions. "Jim... Rick Rose. He's our new mouth mechanic."

My dad would have been upset to learn that after all those years, and all that money, I was being referred to as a mechanic. What the hell, it had a better ring than forensic odontologist.

Jim held out his hand. "Hey, Rick. Hear you're a virgin."

"I beg your pardon?"

"Ya know, your first time in the morgue."

"Oh. Yeah, first time."

"Ya ever see a dead body?"

It wasn't rocket science to see what this guy was doing, so I did my best not to look stupid. "Sure, we took one apart for two semesters in my freshman year."

Jim started to laugh. "No, I mean one that's already been taken apart."

Alex interrupted. "Let's skip the new guy hazing. Okay, Jim?"

"No problem." He tossed his empty coffee cup at the trash, like he was shooting a game-winning free throw, and pumped his fist in the air when the cup landed inside the can. "Let's go inside?" he said.

Alex tapped a four-digit code into the security panel, and the door swung open. The first thing that hit me was the smell—a mixture of formaldehyde, decayed organic matter and Clorox. My breakfast was on the move again. "Is there a men's room nearby?" I asked.

Jim grinned. Alex pointed down the hall. "I'll leave the door ajar," she said.

I figured there was no sense in fighting it; I hung my head over the porcelain and let go. After washing up, I looked in the mirror. I was always proud of my olive complexion, but right then it was a shade of gray I'd never seen.

I headed back to the morgue and, as promised, the door had been left open a crack. I stepped inside just in time to see Alex push Jim's hand away from her butt.

The interior looked exactly the way it does in the movies—lots of stainless and rows of drawers, either waiting for or housing bodies. There were two portable x-ray machines and four operating tables; only one was in use. The guy at the end of it was dressed in full surgical garb and standing next to him were Alex and Jim, both wearing masks and gloves. I coughed to announce my arrival.

Alex looked up. "Rick, put on some gear and join us."

I did as I was asked and approached the table where the body was laid out. "Ya bring any donuts?" Jim asked. Alex shot him an icy look. He held up his palms. "Hey, I'm only kiddin'. Okay?"

I didn't think it was possible, but the corpse made the photos look like passport pictures. The man at the foot of the table, who looked a little like Count Dracula in a mask, didn't bother to introduce himself. His nameplate read: *Dr. H. Reingold*. He looked directly at me, wedged two fingers from each hand between the patient's jaws and pulled the mouth open. "We'll need a full dental checkup, complete with x-rays," he blurted.

It took me aback. "Now?" I asked.

"Of course, not now. You can have the body any time after noon tomorrow."

I turned to Jim. "I'll need a dental assistant. You busy?"

Now, it was Jim's turn to look a little pale. "Uh...yeah...sorry."

"No stomach for it, eh big guy?"

"No, that ain't it at all. I have an important interview tomorrow with a... a perp in a case I'm working on."

I was pretty sure no one in the room believed him, and I was pretty sure he knew it. He sheepishly looked at Alex. "Honest," he said. His voice still lacked conviction.

Even with her mask on, I thought I saw a smile in Alex's eyes. She said, "I'll be glad to assist you, Dr Rose." She turned to Jim. "Detective, do you have your prelim report completed?"

"Well, I ...I ...actually I haven't started it yet."

"And why is that?"

"I've been busy."

Alex's eyes narrowed, and it was obvious she was pissed. "The rule is a prelim within twenty-four hours. You're already a day late," she said.

I wasn't sure if that was a dressing down or a lover's quarrel, but Alex cleared up any ambiguity. "Nine o'clock tomorrow morning, on my desk or off the case." Jim gave her a perfunctory nod.

Alex snapped off her mask and gloves and tossed them on the floor near his feet. "Nine o'clock ...sharp." She walked out of the room.

I was sure the guys wanted me to hang around for some quality male bonding time, but kumbaya wasn't really my thing. I followed Alex up the stairs.

The office door was half open, and it was my intention to knock before entering; Alex spotted me before I had a chance. "Rick, come in," she said. "And close the door behind you." I did as I was told, and Alex motioned to the chair facing her desk. "So, how do you like it so far?"

My instincts told me to trust Alex, but I didn't have a good read on her yet, hence I didn't know if I should be truthful or sugar-coat my answer. I took a chance. "Alex, this place is a fuckin' snake pit."

She broke out laughing. "I apologize. I should have warned you before taking you into the inner sanctum."

"That's okay, but what's with that Reingold guy?"

"Oh, him. Actually, he's a brilliant doctor, number one at Stanford Med, but he has no people skills, so he went into pathology. It suits him well." The wall clock chimed noon and Alex glanced in its direction. "I owe you for this morning. How about I spring for lunch?"

The cab dropped us off in the middle of the financial district and we walked the block and a half to the Tadich Grill. If you've lived in San Francisco, visited the city, or just passed through it, you've probably eaten at Tadich's. It's reputed to be the oldest restaurant in California, with the best seafood in the state and the rudest waiters in the universe. Our guy took the order while he looked around the room and nodded to his regulars. When I asked if tartar sauce came with the Petrale Sole, he told me I might be happier going to Long John Silver's.

Alex sipped from a martini glass, and I sucked Diet Pepsi through a straw as we dug into the fish. "Your detective friend is an asshole," I said.

She cracked just a hint of a smile. "I admit he can be annoying, but he's worked on a lot of cases for us. I'd humor him a little. He just might come in handy one day."

"Thanks for the advice, but he's still a jerk." I didn't want to ruin our lunch by talking about a macho cop with a hard-on for my boss, so I changed the subject. "Tell me more about the case."

Alex ran the martini toothpick between her lips to get at the olive. "Well, I haven't seen the initial report yet, but it's not every day that a guy dressed for the opera ends up dead in a dumpster with no ID and no traceable prints."

I took the last bite of my grilled fish. It was delicious even without the tartar sauce. "Where do I fit in?"

"First, we need to identify this guy, then maybe we can figure out why he was killed and, if we're lucky, by whom. Do a good exam and get us something—something for us to start with."

"Were you serious about assisting me?"

"Were you serious about needing an assistant?"

My glass was empty, and the waiter apparently wasn't interested in re-filling it, so I worked an ice cube out of the glass and began sucking on it. "Yeah, I could use your help."

"Okay, I'll meet you in the morgue tomorrow at one o'clock." Alex looked around for the waiter to deliver the check, but he was too busy having a drink at the bar with one of his buddies.

Three

After we left the restaurant, Alex and I headed in different directions. She took a cab back to the office down near the waterfront, and I jumped in an Uber pointed up the hill on Jackson Street. I mentioned earlier that my new apartment was in the Pacific Heights neighborhood. What I didn't make clear was that, with its unique location and spectacular views of the bay, it's one of the most desirable areas of the city.

When the driver reached the top of the hill, he came to a screeching stop. It appears several foreign countries house their dignitaries in mansions in Pacific Heights, and one of them was apparently hosting a social function. "What's the problem?" I asked.

"Goddamn foreigners. They can't speak no English, and they park their fancy cars in d'middle of the road." I couldn't help but notice that my driver had a heavy accent and was obviously from another country, but I guess he didn't include himself as a foreigner; most likely he already had his green card.

The Uber prick managed to break free of the bottleneck and, two blocks later, deposited me on the 1700 block of Jackson Street. I tapped a fifty-cent tip into the app and waved goodbye.

My apartment was the top floor of an old Victorian which had been built in 1908, two years after the earthquake. I still couldn't believe my luck—thirty-two hundred a month for a view of Alcatraz, the Golden Gate Bridge, and the Marin headlands.

I killed time while waiting for five o'clock to arrive. In my previous life, at the end of a day like today, I'd pour myself a martini or maybe a Jack Daniels on the rocks, but I settled for a Perrier with a twist. My diversion counselor would have been proud of his work.

I was sitting on the deck, drinking my cocktail and looking out at the view, when my cell phone buzzed. I recognized the ID. "Please hold for the doctor," I answered.

"Rick, is that you?"

I hadn't talked to my ex-wife in almost a year. "Yeah, Josie, it's me." This was one of those times I wished I had failed rehab. The sparkling water just didn't cut it. "Hey, how're you doing?"

"I'm doing fine. You?"

"Other than losing my license, my practice and the house, things are great."

"Gosh, I didn't know. Is there anything I can do?"

I wanted to say yes, you can mail the cat back to me, but instead I said, "No, I'm good."

"Are you working?" she asked.

"Yeah, try to Google me. I'm the forensic odontologist for San Francisco."

"Wow, I'm impressed."

"Don't be. I think I was the only one dumb enough to apply for the job. So why this call out of the blue?"

"I think I'd like to have a baby."

"Well, I think I'd like to be with a super-model on a beach in Maui, but that's not going to happen, so tell me again why you called."

"I'd like you to donate your sperm."

Josie always had a quirky side to her. I used to think it was cute and was one of the things that attracted me to her. But after she left me in the lurch, it lost its allure, and I figured she just wasn't firing on all cylinders. I said, "You're too late. I've already donated."

"Hear me out. I went to a fertility specialist, and he thinks he can inseminate me."

"Fine, let him inseminate you. I've already tried and it didn't work."

"Would you consider it?"

"I don't get it. Do you want us to do the deed or do you want me to just mail it to you in a test tube?"

"Come on, Rick, you're making it sound dirty. I want a baby, and I want it to be a Rosenkofsky."

"Then maybe you should ask my father."

"I'm serious. Will you at least come with me and meet Dr. Rosenberg? Please."

I was getting a real headache and felt like I needed another shot of Perrier, but I didn't want to get addicted. "I'll think about it. Call me in a couple days."

"Promise me you will ...you'll think about it?"

I would have said anything to end that conversation, so I did. "I promise."

Four

Alex had agreed to meet me in the morgue at one o'clock, but I needed some time to acclimate. I got there at noon. Reingold was finishing the cleanup of John Doe, and I have to admit he looked a lot better—John Doe, I mean.

"Good afternoon, Dr. Rose," Reingold said.

"Oh, hi. Say, Doctor, my first name's Rick. What's yours?"

"Helmut, but everyone calls me Dr. Reingold."

"How 'bout you call me Rick and I'll call you Helmut?"

Reingold began to fidget and his upper lip broke out with a couple beads of perspiration. "I ... I guess that would be all right."

"Great. So, Helmut, what am I dealing with here?"

I could tell he was still digesting this first name thing, but I was pretty sure he could handle it. He said, "First, I ...I want to apologize for my rudeness yesterday. It's just ...just hard for me to...

I didn't like watching him struggle, so I interrupted. "It's okay, I understand we all can't be Dale Carnegie graduates. Your strength is right here in this lab and, from what I hear, you're great at it."

"Thanks ...Rick. What do you want to know?"

"Just give me some background, so I can figure out what I'm looking for."

"Okay, sure. You probably know John Doe was left in a dumpster. He'd been badly beaten, and I'm guessing he died from a brain hemorrhage, but we won't know for sure until I do the autopsy. The strange thing, though, is his mouth. It's messed up in a way that's not ...not consistent with your usual beating."

"What d'ya mean, not consistent?"

"Well, he had the usual marks. He was swollen around the eyes and cheeks, with a lot of bruising and bleeding, just what you'd expect if someone was beaten to death, but his mouth— you'll see. It was worked over pretty well."

"Okay, I'll check it out. Say, I'm going to need casts of the victim's mouth. Did the last dent..." I was going to say dentist, but apparently that wasn't appropriate around here, so I started to say mouth mechanic, but out of respect for my dad I couldn't do it. Instead, I said, "Did the last odont' guy leave any impression material?"

Helmut nodded. "Yes, I think he did. I'll get it for you."

I thanked him and went over to the table. As I said, Helmut did a fine job of making John Doe presentable, even though it was quite obvious he wouldn't be attending any social functions in the near future. I could see what Helmut was talking about; John's lips were a mess. They were split open as if someone tried to push a square block through a round opening.

Helmut had positioned a Siemens portable x-ray machine next to the body. It was state of the art; much better than the one

I sold when I liquidated my office. I checked the settings and fine-tuned the numbers just before the front door opened, and Alex stepped in. "That was a great lunch yesterday," she said.

"It sure was. I forgot to thank you."

She waved it off. "I put it on the expense account. We ready?"

We both put on surgical scrubs, masks and gloves before touching the table where John was lying. I explained to Alex that this x-ray machine was digital, meaning instead of using photographic films we were going to use sensors to pick up the images and transfer them onto a computer.

In my old office, patients would either bite down on the sensors or use their fingers to hold them in place while the technician would operate the x-ray machine from about six feet away. In this case, I didn't have the luxury of a cooperative patient, so I dug up a set of extenders which allowed me to hold the sensors in place from a distance. It seemed like a good idea until I realized I still couldn't get more than two feet away from the radiation. I dug up a shoulder-to-ankle lead apron and draped it over me. It crossed my mind that the risk I was taking might put a damper on Josie's future plans, but I wasn't about to lose any sleep over it.

One at a time, I positioned each sensor into John's mouth, gave the high sign to Alex, and she snapped the x-ray. It took eighteen shots to get images of all the teeth.

"Rick, this is really interesting," Alex said. "I've been on this job for almost ten years and this is the first time I've seen up close what a forensic dentist does."

"Well, this is just the beginning. Ready to do the exam?"

"Sure. I want to see more."

I handed Alex a generic dental chart. "I'll call out tooth numbers and give you details. Your job is to check the appropriate boxes next to each one." While going through my routine, just as I did when I was in practice, I kept a conversation going with my assistant. "So, Alex, I'm a little curious. What happened to the last dentist who worked here?"

"He retired. Thank God."

"What? He was no good?"

"He was eighty-one when he retired—very old school. Rick, I'm re-building this department. Look around, we're all millennials. No one's much over forty, and we're all up to date with today's techniques and challenges."

"So, I'm thirty-five. Is that why my credentials were so impressive?"

"Pretty much."

"Huh, and I thought the fact that I ranked ninety-first out of a class of a hundred was what sealed the deal."

Helmut popped his head into our conversation. "Hey, Rick, I'll set this impression material on the tray ...oh, and I arranged with a lab to make the plaster casts for you."

I thanked him and went back to work. It was tough working on a dead patient; it took almost an hour to finish the exam and another twenty minutes just to take the impressions. The only redeeming factor was that he wasn't salivating all over me like my previous patients had a habit of doing.

Alex and I removed the protective gear and began washing up. "I'll start looking over these images at home tonight," I said.

"You don't have to do that. Tomorrow's soon enough."

I dried my hands. "Hey, I'm a millennial. This is how we do it."

Five

I transferred all the x-rays and exam data to a flash drive and slipped it into my pocket. The xenophobe I rode with yesterday had pissed me off, so I decided to boycott Uber. I hailed a Yellow Cab. I liked this guy. He had his earbuds in and made no attempt at conversation.

Just like the day before, when we reached the top of the hill, traffic was snarled by limos and fancy town cars double-parked in front of one of the classical Victorian mansions. I tapped the driver's shoulder to get his attention; he turned around with his eyes open way too wide. I guess he had forgotten I was in the back seat. "I'll walk the rest of the way," I said. I added an extra three bucks to the tab and headed up Jackson Street.

I was curious what kind of shindig was going on in this mansion, so I decided to take a look. As I got closer, I realized all the vehicles were chauffeur-driven and most of the drivers were in uniform, standing at parade rest next to their shiny black behemoths.

It was an odd lineup. All the Cadillacs were in the back of the line and all the Mercedes were in the front. I approached the nearest Cadillac driver, feeling skeptical that he would break ranks for a conversation with a commoner. "Hey, how're you doing?" I asked.

To my surprise he smiled. "I'm fine. You?"

"Yeah, good." I pointed to the mansion. "Geez, that's a big house. Who owns it?"

"I don't know who owns it, but the Saudis are using it."

Geography wasn't one of my prerequisites for dental school. "You mean like in Arabia?"

The chauffeur laughed. "Yeah, you got it—Saudi Arabia."

"Man, they're a long way from home. What's with all the cars?"

"Beats me, but whatever's going on, it's been going for about a week."

"So, you don't work for them?" I asked.

"Nah, they rent both the limo and me for the day to pick up guests." He pointed ahead. "But those drivers up front are all Saudi guys. I'm not sure what they're doin.'"

I patted the hood. "Nice car. Maybe I'll get me one." I gave kind of a salute and moved on.

When I reached the Mercedes near the front of the line, I noticed the drivers weren't in uniforms or standing at attention. They were just huddled together smoking cigarettes. They appeared friendly enough, so I approached one of them and thought I'd use the same intro I used with the Cadillac guy. "Hey, how're you doing?" He didn't so much as turn to see who was talking. I thought I'd change it up a little. "So, how're you doing?"

This time he turned. "Who's asking?"

"Just a fan of the Saudis'."

"Fuck off."

I sensed the conversation wasn't going well and then realized it was about to get worse. A guy who looked like he could go fifteen rounds with Rocky Balboa was running in my direction. "Hey, you!" he yelled.

I looked behind me, hoping he was addressing someone else, but no such luck. I weighed my options and came up with a weak, "Hi."

He grabbed the front of my shirt. "What're you doin' here?"

"Just looking at all the cars."

"Yeah, well there's an agency on Market Street. You can look at them there." He let go of my shirt. "Now get the hell outta here."

I held up both palms and backed away. "Sure. No problem. See ya." As I stepped away, I noticed a squad of belligerent-looking guys stationed around the perimeter of the Victorian structure.

Six

Some people are night people; they never turn in before two a.m. I wasn't one of them. After eleven, my lids would get heavy, and I would tend to doze off. It was well after midnight by the time I viewed all the x-rays and my neck was sore from my head listing to the side and snapping back to its upright position. I couldn't take it any longer and fell asleep at my desk with my clothes on.

I had a dream, or should I say a nightmare. I was back with Josie, and we wanted a baby, and we were trying to get somewhere, but there was an obstacle. We pushed it aside and just when we thought we could get to where we were going, something else would stand in our way. Finally, we reached a door and opened it. We were in a medical office and a doctor stepped into the room. It was Dr. Reingold. I woke with a start.

My computer was still on. I checked the time. It was after nine o'clock. Alex never said what time I should show up in the morning; if she had, I was pretty sure it wouldn't have been after ten. I ran through a shower, didn't bother to shave, and skipped breakfast. I ended my boycott of Uber and jumped in one heading downtown. I went running through the medical examiner's office door at 10:45.

Alex's secretary looked up from her computer. "Oh, hello Dr. Rose. Dr. Keller is expecting you. Go right in." I stepped into her office and realized I may be faced with my first major decision as the forensic odontologist for the City and County of San Francisco. Do I tell Alex the truth or do I make up a lie?

She looked at her watch. "Should I ask?"

I said "No." And that was that.

"I found you a corner office," Alex said.

"Is that good?"

"It's a two-holer."

It sounded like a prison cell. I kind of cocked my head like our cat, or should I say like Josie's cat, used to do. "A what?"

Alex tried to hold back a laugh, but it leaked out. "Two windows—get it?"

I nodded and felt like the rookie I was. "Yeah, I get it. I guess I'll have to spend some time learning bureaucracy jargon."

Her laugh melted into that warm smile I had seen at our first meeting. "Rick, you're doing great. The way you handled the exam yesterday was impressive, so don't think you need to spend your valuable time learning some useless vocabulary. I think what you really need is a cup of coffee. You look like hell."

There was a carafe on the table and Alex poured two cups. "Cream ...sugar?" she asked.

"Black's fine ...two sugars."

We sat and drank coffee while Alex talked. I heard a little of what she said, but most of it was lost. I was mesmerized by the sound of her voice. It was soft, it was caring, and it made me feel relaxed, like listening to a Mozart concerto.

"So, what do you think?" she said.

I snapped out of my trance with absolutely no clue. "Fine, that's fine," I said.

"What's fine?"

"Uh, the two-holer. I'll set up my stuff in there right away." She had a sort of quizzical look on her face, and I was pretty sure she was questioning her decision to hire me; if she wasn't, she should have. My saving grace was that I was only thirty-five, and I figured that trumped being a total idiot.

The office was great. It had a big desk with a new HP computer and an Epson printer. There were a little couch and a couple chairs and, as Alex promised, it had two holes—both covered with pleated blinds. The best perk was that it came with a private secretary—a sweet young woman named Stella.

I retrieved the flash drive and my written notes from the briefcase that was given to me by my parents on the day I graduated. I felt my gut tighten. I hadn't told them about my divorce, the diversion program or my practice. If I had, I was sure the first words out of my father's mouth would have been, "Oh, my God, two hundred and fifty thousand?"

I decided to let the guilt train leave without me. Instead, I called down to the morgue where Dr. Reingold answered. "Helmut ...it's Rick. How's it going?

"Oh ...hello, Rick. It's going fine. I've finished the autopsy on our John Doe."

"That's good. Hey, I was wondering when I could get those casts that were made from the impressions I took."

"Oh, they're here. The dental lab dropped them off an hour ago."

"Great, I'll be right down."

I didn't have the same affinity for exercise as Alex did. I took the elevator down to the morgue. Alex had given me my own four-digit code for the door, and I tapped it in. It instilled in me a sense of inclusion—like getting a key to the executive washroom.

Helmut was taking a break from whatever gory project he had planned for today. He pointed to a box on his desk. "They're all yours."

I opened the box and inspected the casts, while he looked on. "They look good," I said.

"The ones with the teeth look fine, but what's that funny looking one?" he asked.

"Oh, that? The chin had a weird look to it, so I thought I'd just impress it too. Did you notice anything?"

"Not really, just cuts and bruises."

I put the casts back in the box and started for the door. "Yeah, that's probably all it was.

Seven

Before I left the office for home, I made an appointment to meet with Alex at nine o'clock the next morning. It would be my first report as the forensic odontologist and, after my tardiness of a couple days ago, I didn't want to be known as 'that guy who's always late,' so I arrived at seven-thirty to prepare.

I brought all the digital x-rays up on my desktop and lined the plaster casts next to the computer. I was also planning on printing out a summary of my findings for everyone on the team, but I thought twice about it and decided to run it by Alex first.

I hadn't given a case presentation since my last year at UCLA. I thought I'd be nervous, but that didn't happen. Unlike those dreaded meetings with professors, where I was uninformed and ill-prepared, on this one I had total command of what I knew and what I was going to say.

The intercom buzzed, and Stella asked, "Dr. Rose, are you ready for Dr. Keller?"

"Sure, anytime."

Alex peeked her head around the door, and I waved her in. "Hey, you're the boss here. Since when do you need permission to see me?"

"Just respecting your space. So, any luck?"

"I think so. Take a look at these x-rays."

She came around to my side of the desk, pulled up a chair and peered at my computer screen. I could tell by her blank look that dental x-rays were not her expertise, but I wasn't about to make myself look good by making her look bad, so I said, "Forgive me if I tell you stuff you may already know..."

"No, that's fine. You're the expert in the room. Let's hear it."

I brushed my hand across the screen. "If we take a macro view of John's mouth, something odd jumps right out. You see it, by any chance?"

"Well, I see a lot of metal in the back of his lower left jaw."

"Yeah, that's true, but it's broader than that. The area with all the metal that you see is where John's left second molar used to be. Other than missing that tooth, this guy had a perfect dentition. He didn't have any decay, he didn't have any fillings, he didn't have any tartar, and he didn't have any bone loss around his teeth—this guy was a poster boy for good dental health."

Alex pointed to the metal. "Except—"

"Except for that one tooth. That thick metal post you see inside the bone is an implant. It's there to replace the missing molar's roots."

"Okay, so?"

"So, where is the crown that was placed on top of that implant, and why would a guy with a perfect dentition lose that tooth in the first place?"

"I'll bite... no pun intended. Why?"

"I think that tooth may have been intentionally removed and replaced with an implant and a crown."

"But there is no crown."

"No, not when we examined him, because it was yanked off with something like a vise grips or big pliers or some other crude instrument."

"How can you tell…?"

I picked up the plaster casts and handed them to Alex. "You can see the crown is missing, but look at the imprint of the gums around the implant. The impressions picked up deep grooves from some tool, and I'm guessing it was large, because the user tore John's lips apart just to get it in there."

I could tell Alex was processing. "So, we have to find out who placed the implant to figure out who this guy was, and why his crown was important enough to kill him for it," she said.

"That's what I'm thinking."

"How?"

"I'm going back into John's mouth and cut that implant out. Then, we'll contact the company who manufactured it."

"I'll have Dr. Reingold schedule you a time. Can I assist?"

I acted surprised, but I knew she would ask. "Absolutely."

She picked up her notebook and started for the door. "Hey, Alex," I said. She turned. "Take a seat, there's more."

Alex settled back into a chair and waited for an explanation. I passed her the plaster cast of John Doe's chin area. She examined it and held up her hands. "What am I looking for here?"

I took a magnifying glass from my drawer and handed it to her. "Here, try this."

She closed one eye to inspect the cast. "There's a dent in the skin."

"Look closer."

She moved the lens in and out. "It's an imprint ...kinda looks like a star."

I nodded. "Most likely made by a ring worn on the pinky finger of the guy who beat him to death."

"How can you tell it was on the pinky?"

I reached into my briefcase and thumbed through my copies of John Doe's photographs. When I found the one I was looking for, I laid it next to the plaster cast and pointed to John's chin. "If you look closely at this photo, you can make out that star you see on the cast."

Alex lifted the photo and squinted as she examined it. "Yes, I see it."

"What do you see to the left of it?" I asked.

She focused the magnifying glass on the photo. "Three bruises lined up in a row."

I took my ballpoint and drew a star on my little finger where a ring would go and then drew a circle around each of my other three knuckles. Then I made a fist and held it up in front of her. "Three knuckles and a ring worn on the pinky finger of a right hand would fit that pattern perfectly."

Alex placed the photo next to the cast. "Interesting," she said. "Rick, this is really good work. I want you to run it by the team."

I have to say, for the first time in quite a while, I was proud of myself.

Eight

The next day I arrived at the office before eight and found a memo on my desk from Dr. Alexandra Keller. It was titled *John Doe team meeting 10:00 a.m.* with a c.c. to Dr. Rick Rose, Dr. Helmut Reingold and Detective James Allen. It gave me a warm and fuzzy feeling to see that I had moved two spots ahead of Jim. It didn't seem to bother him. Before the meeting began, he waved across the table and grinned. "Hey, Doc, how's it goin'?"

Alex gave the pre-game speech. "This isn't our usual dead guy in a dumpster case. John Doe wasn't homeless; he wasn't a derelict and he wasn't a drug addict. His wardrobe suggests he was quite affluent. The fact that we can't identify him also suggests–either he, his killer, or both, didn't want his identity known."

Since I was in the number two position, I was next to give a summary of my findings. When I gave my theory for why John was missing that lower second molar, Jim's mood changed. "I think our new doc has seen too many episodes of CSI," he said. "I get it, he's a newbie, but come on. He's suggesting some sinister shit that probably doesn't even exist. John Doe was beaten, robbed and tossed in that dumpster. A rich guy in the wrong place at the wrong time."

My inclination was to defend my opinion, but Jim was right about one thing: I was a newbie. Maybe I was dramatizing to make myself relevant. On the other hand, maybe I was right, and there was something sinister at play. I decided to shut up, figuring time would tell who was right and who was wrong.

Helmut summarized his general autopsy findings. His previous inclination proved to be correct; the cause of death was trauma to the brain. His report ignored John Doe's dental condition and made no mention of the imprint on the tissue of his chin.

Jim's preliminary report was brief. He stated that there were no suspects at the present time and if his robbery theory were correct, there probably would be no suspects in the future. He said he was going back to the dumpster this afternoon to make sure he hadn't missed anything when he'd answered the homicide call five days ago.

"Can I go with you?" I asked.

He looked at me like I had just arrived from a ninth planet in the solar system. "Why?" he said.

"I'm new. I'd like to see how a pro does it."

"Yeah, well, I don't need you nosing around and asking me a bunch of stupid questions."

In the movies, the cop is always a sucker for a free meal, so I said, "Lunch ...I'll buy."

To my surprise it worked. "That include a beer?" he asked.

"Absolutely," I said.

I made arrangements to meet Jim in the dumpster alley at noon, then I headed to the break room for a cup of coffee. I indulged myself with a stale jelly donut and checked the time. It was a few minutes before eleven; I decided to drop in on Alex.

Alex's door was closed, but I couldn't help but hear that an argument was going on inside. I retreated to the end of the hall just as the door opened and Jim stormed out. "Bitch!" he shouted. He slammed the door and stomped off in the opposite direction.

I tapped lightly on Alex's door. "I told you to stay the hell outta here," she yelled.

I was pretty sure the order wasn't meant for me, so I tapped again. "Alex? It's me, Rick."

There was a pause, and then she opened the door. Her expression was a mix of anger and sadness. "Oh, Rick. I'm so sorry, I thought you were someone else."

"Is this a bad time?" I asked.

She forced a smile. "No ...no, it's fine. Come in."

The silence was awkward, and I knew it was none of my business, but I said, "I saw Jim leave. Can I help?"

"I appreciate it, Rick. I do, but I think not."

I nodded and pivoted to the real reason I was there. "Are you okay with me shadowing Jim to the scene?"

"Sure, I'm fine with it. He's a twenty-year man and doesn't always see what he doesn't want to see. A fresh set of eyes can't hurt."

"Okay, great. Would you like to join us?"

She smirked. "I don't think so. I've had enough of James Allen for one day."

I felt I had already overstepped my bounds. "Sure, I get it. I'll let you know how it goes."

The Mouth Mechanic

~ * ~

The Stinking Rose was named for the chief ingredient used in all its dishes and when I stepped into the alley behind the restaurant, there was no question what the ingredient was. It smelled like the blacktop was basted in garlic.

Jim was already there, along with another detective who looked about twelve years old. Jim introduced him as a trainee, whatever that meant. The guy said about two words the entire time we were there.

It had been five days since John Doe had rolled out of the dumpster and by now the restaurant's bin was overflowing again. I was worried Jim would send his trainee into the garlic pit, but he didn't. Instead, they walked the alley together and kicked at debris that was strewn around. After a wasted half hour, Jim bummed a cigarette from the young man, and they both headed back to the car.

I don't why, but I hung around the alley trying to create a picture in my mind of a well-dressed John Doe being dropped into the dumpster. I heard a noise and looked up. A shabbily dressed guy pushing a grocery cart filled with junk came into the alley and began doing a better job of checking it out than the detectives had.

I approached him. "Hey, buddy, how're you doing?"

The man looked around and realized he may have wandered into a place he shouldn't have. He did an about face and headed for the exit. "Hey, wait. You're okay," I said.

"I don't want any t ...trouble," he said.

"You're not in any trouble. Can I ask you a few questions?"

The guy didn't answer and began pushing his cart toward the end of the alley. I took out a ten-dollar bill and handed it to him. "Please, just a few questions." He took the bill and waited. "Do you come here often?" I asked.

He nodded in the affirmative. "They throw out a lot of g ...good stuff."

"So, sometimes you come here after the restaurant closes?"

The guy nodded. "Every night."

"So, four nights ago, were you here?" He nodded again. "Did you see anything unusual?"

The homeless have a radar of their own; they sense when they may be in jeopardy. The guy left his cart and began to stumble for the exit. I ran after him and grabbed his arm. "You're not in trouble. Just tell me what you saw. Please."

It wasn't a good feeling to see a grown man scared, and this man was terrified. His hands began to tremble and he began to stutter. "I didn't s...see anything."

I grabbed hold of his cart and began walking it to the end of the alley. "Come with me," I said. We left the alley and started up Columbus Avenue. When we were a block away from the scene I asked, "What did you see?"

"A big b...black Mercedes car. It came into the a...alley, and they dropped a man into the d...dumpster."

"The Mercedes car. What can you remember about it?"

"People think I'm s...stupid, but I'm not. I remember everything."

"What do you remember about the car?"

"It was like a b ...big station wagon."

"You mean an SUV?"

"That's it ...SUV."

"What else?"

"One of the in ...insignias on the back had the letters, GLS 600."

I reached into my pocket, and all I had was a twenty. I handed it to the guy. "Thanks, buddy. By the way, my name's Rick. What's yours?"

"It's Gabriel, but you can c ...call me Gabe."

I clutched his shoulder and said, "Stay safe out there, Gabe."

I made my way back toward the alley. Jim and his trainee were still sitting in their car smoking cigarettes. "What was that all about?" Jim asked.

I shook my head. "Nothing, just a homeless guy looking for some food. Hey, let's get out of here. I owe you guys a lunch."

Nine

That evening while I sipped on an alcohol-free martini, I began thinking about the afternoon. Something didn't smell right about that alley behind the Stinking Rose, and I'm not talking about the garlic. It was a little after ten—still an hour before my bedtime—so I thought I'd take another look during night time hours.

Parking places are non-existent in San Francisco—that's why I put my car in drydock outside the city for three months. I decided to go back to boycotting Uber, so I used the Lyft app instead. The guy was at my front door in four minutes and during the ride to North Beach he didn't talk politics, current events, or immigration. I tipped him five dollars in cash so he wouldn't have to report it to the company.

North Beach at night is a different place than North Beach in the afternoon. The streets were packed with droves of tourists and a spattering of locals, all checking out the bars, restaurants, and topless joints. The seedier establishments had barkers out front doing their best to entice people to step inside.

My Lyft guy dropped me at the corner of Broadway and Columbus—the center of the district and less than a block away from the restaurant—and I used my nose to lead me the rest of the way. The alley entrance was around the corner, right next to a blinking sign of a naked girl with her arms and legs gripping a pole.

The alley itself was much darker than I had envisioned. Its only light came from a single hundred-watt bulb over the restaurant's back door. The dumpster itself was pretty much unlit. While I was scoping it out, a head popped up from inside. It was my confidential source from the afternoon visit. When he saw me, he ducked back into the dumpster.

"Hey, Gabe, it's me, Rick."

His head slowly reappeared. "Hi, Rick. How 'bout some dinner. The special's g ...garlic lasagna tonight."

"No thanks, but jump outta there, and I'll take you for a dessert."

Gabe knew the area well and directed us to a small coffee house that baked its own sweets. I ordered a Napoleon and a double decaf espresso. Gabe, who admitted it had been three years since he was last inside a restaurant, did the same.

The baked goods were outrageous, and I wolfed mine down faster than my guest, then we slowed down to drink the coffee. "I didn't tell you everything this afternoon," Gabe said.

"How come?" I asked.

"I didn't trust you."

I noticed Gabe's stutter had disappeared. "Do you want to tell me now?"

He took a sugar cube off his saucer and popped it into his mouth. "I think I do," he said. I didn't respond—just let his thoughts percolate a little. "That guy you were with ...he's a bad guy."

"How so?"

"He beats up hookers."

"How do you know?"

"I've seen him bring them into my alley to get a B.J. and when they're done, he smacks them around instead of paying them."

I signaled the waitress for refills on our espressos. "What about the night that guy was thrown into the dumpster? Was he there that night?"

Gabe took a sip from the hot coffee. "Yeah, he was there earlier, but he hightailed it outta there about an hour before the Mercedes showed up."

"What about a hooker?"

"I'm not sure. I didn't see one."

I looked at my watch, and it was almost midnight. I shook Gabe's hand. "I have to go. Thanks for the info." I handed him a twenty.

He held up his palm. "No. No handouts from friends."

I put the bill back into my pocket. "That's cool, but how about I put you on my payroll?" I handed him my card. "This is my cell phone. If you see anything strange around that alley, give me a buzz. Twenty bucks a call. Deal?"

He grinned. "Deal."

Ten

Dr. Reingold put me on the dissection schedule for nine-thirty the next day. I guess it's true that after a while you can get used to anything. This was my third visit to the morgue, and it was beginning to feel normal to be surrounded by dead people. Even the odors that made me puke a few days earlier seemed almost tolerable.

I have to admit, Helmut ran a good ship. When I arrived, John was already on the operating table, and all the instruments were sterilized and placed in sealed bags. "Is there anything else you will need, Dr. Rose?" Helmut asked.

I waved a finger in the air. "Rick, it's Rick. Remember?"

"Yes, of course. Anything else, Rick?"

I took a quick inventory. "I'll need a rotary bone saw that will fit on the end of the dental drill."

"No problem," he said and scurried off.

Even though I was sort of getting used to the place, that didn't mean I wanted to spend a lot of time there. I looked at my watch. It was nine forty-five. Alex was late. When the digits on the wall clock clicked from 9:59 to 10:00, I phoned her.

She answered on the first ring. "Alex, it's Rick," I said. "I'm with John, and we're waiting for you."

"Oh, my God. I'll be down in five minutes."

Alex came bursting through the door. She looked terrible. Her eyes were puffy as if she had been crying, and there were bags underneath, signaling a lack of sleep. "I'm so sorry," she said. She pulled her protective gear on over her street clothes and stepped to the table.

"Are you all right?" I asked

"Fine. I'm fine," she said.

I summarized the procedure we had planned for John. I explained that we would retract the soft tissue and remove sections of the lower jaw bone that housed the implant. For obvious reasons, sutures wouldn't be necessary.

I was about to make the first cut, but I set the scalpel back on the tray. "Alex, do you want to talk about it?"

"The procedure?"

"No, you. You're not yourself. Maybe just getting it off your chest would help." In that instant, I became aware that having a conversation with a dead body present wasn't the best environment to work out emotional problems. "This procedure can wait," I said. "Let's get rid of this gear and go up the street for some coffee."

There's not a Starbucks in the world that isn't crowded at ten-thirty in the morning. We spotted a couple seats in the back, and Alex made a beeline for them while I waited in line for two mochas. I set the cups on the table, and we each took a few sips while the coffee cooled down. "So ...do you want to unload?"

"Just a lover's quarrel."

I really didn't know Alex that well, but I was pretty sure that just a spat with her boyfriend wouldn't send her into emotional turmoil. "Really, that's all?"

Alex forced a smile and put her hand over mine. "That's all ...but Rick, I'm grateful for your caring."

I couldn't for the life of me figure out why a classy, professional woman like Alex would have a romantic relationship with such a self-centered, uneducated prick like Jim. But I knew the answer to the question wouldn't help Alex out of her predicament, so I classified it in my brain's useless information section.

I told Alex I could handle the operation on John Doe without her help and suggested she take the rest of the day off to pull herself together. She agreed and grabbed a cab going uptown, while I went back to the inner sanctum and removed the implant.

Helmut was there when I finished. I showed him the dissected material. "Do you have a chemical that will dissolve the bone away from this implant without damaging it?" I asked.

"Is it titanium?"

"Should be."

Helmut took the specimens and dropped them into a beaker. "Twenty percent sulfuric acid should work. It'll take about 24 hours."

Eleven

I arrived back at my apartment at cocktail hour. I had already decided to discard Perrier for something stronger, so I opened a bottle of tonic, poured it over ice, squeezed in a fresh lime and topped it with a bright red Maraschino cherry. It was delicious.

My apartment had a deck just big enough for a three-foot round table and two cushioned chairs. There was no fog for a change, so I grabbed my drink and my MacBook Pro and settled into the chair facing the bay.

I opened the laptop and googled Mercedes GLS 600. The flagship of the fleet was an SUV named Maybach GLS 600 4MATIC. It began production early this year and didn't reach the showrooms until the middle of August. That was only two months ago.

My phone buzzed, and I checked the ID. "Shit," I mumbled. My inclination was to let it go to voicemail, but because there had been some good times along with the bad, I answered. "Brain surgery department. Can I help you?"

"Come on, Rick, cut the jokes."

"Okay. So, Josie, I assume you're calling about the sperm delivery."

"Rick ..."

"I can't do it."

"Why?"

"Because I don't want to."

"That's not a good reason."

"Okay, then it's bizarre. Who wants an ex-husband to father their child?"

"I do and it's not bizarre. It's a compliment."

"I don't need any compliments. Hey, I have an important call coming in. Can I call you right back?"

"Sure, I'll stand by the phone."

I hung up, turned my cell to silent mode and went back to my computer. I tried to get the sales figures for the Maybach GLS600, but it was too new; however, with a sticker price of over $200,000, it was my guess there weren't many of them on the road.

Twelve

The next day, I was relaxing behind my desk, reviewing my notes and downing my third cup of coffee, when my phone buzzed. Since I was on the county's clock, I chose to answer in the vernacular. "Dr. Rose, here."

"Hello, Rick, It's Helmut."

"Oh, hey, Helmut. What's up?"

"Your implant is as smooth as a newborn's bottom, and the titanium looks like it was polished with Turtle Wax."

"That's great. I'll be right down."

"No need. My intern is already on his way up to your office. Just sign the chain of custody form. It's evidence, you know."

I knew what chain of custody was. So did everyone else who watched reruns of the O.J. trial. "Will do. Thanks, buddy," I said.

Helmut was right. Besides removing all the organic material, the sulfuric acid had left the implant super shiny. The only problem was, whatever letters or numbers the manufacturer had placed on the implant were gone.

I used the intercom to contact the morgue. Helmut picked up. "Dr. Reingold."

"Helmut, it's Rick."

"Yes, Rick, what can I do for you?"

"I'm checking out that implant, and it looks like the acid may have taken off all the lettering and numbering. Is there any way you can help me?"

"Oh, gosh, I didn't think that would happen. Bring it down, and I'll see what I can do."

Here I was again, headed for the morgue, on a first name basis with a pathologist who was more at ease in the company of the dead than the living. I was beginning to wonder why we got along so well.

I tapped my code and stepped inside. Just like all the pathologists on TV, Helmut was eating his lunch next to the dissection table. He held up half a sandwich. "Hey, Rick, have you eaten?"

I was starved, but ..."Yeah, just finished," I said. "Thanks anyway." I handed him the implant. "What d'ya think?"

He lifted his glasses to get a better look through the bottom of his bifocals and ran his thumbnail across the metal. "I didn't notice it before, but the acid etched the outer surfaces."

"Am I screwed?"

Helmut put the implant in his pocket and motioned me to follow him to a counter where five microscopes were lined up. One of them didn't look anything like the ones we used in dental school. He went straight for it.

"Is that actually a microscope?" I asked.

"Yup, a Zeiss Discovery.V8 Stereo."

"Am I supposed to be impressed?"

"This baby cost ten grand—stripped."

Now I was impressed. "I'm betting it magnifies metal pretty well."

Helmut smiled wider than I'd ever seen him smile. Come to think of it, though, I'd never really seen him smile.

He turned on the high intensity lamp inside the unit and placed the implant under a clip on the stage. He looked through the eyepieces and rotated a knob to focus the image. "Shit," he said.

My eyes opened wide. I didn't think Helmut knew any nasty four-letter words. "What is it?" I asked.

"The etching is really deep. I think I blew it for you."

"Keep checking," I said.

He was looking pretty grim by the time he turned it over for the third time, but he suddenly became animated. "I've got something," he said. "There's a few letters, but they look like some ancient symbols or something." He stepped aside. "Take a look."

I focused the image. They were ancient all right. "These are the Hebrew letters *Chet* and *Yod* that form the word *Chai*. It means life. It's kind of a good luck symbol."

Helmut was downright impressed. "Did they teach you that in dental school?"

"Nope, in Hebrew school. One of the perks of growing up Jewish in Brooklyn." I looked again through the scope. "This implant was manufactured in Israel."

~ * ~

When I checked the catalogs, it became evident that Israel was one of the leading countries for the production of dental implants. Google listed twenty-five manufacturers, most of whom sold to the European markets. I knew I needed to make some long-distance calls, but since my cell phone carrier charged for inter-country minutes, I decided to use the land line that came with my office.

One by one I contacted each manufacturer. None of them confessed to having a *Chai* inscribed on their products and a couple of them appeared annoyed or angry that I even asked. Talia, the manager of the last company on my list, took pity on me. "Are you familiar with the *Chai*?" she asked.

"Well, I know it means life and a lot of people in New York wear big gold ones around their necks."

"Yes, as good luck symbols, but the word goes beyond that. There have been various mystical numerological speculations about the fact that, according to the system of gematria, the letters of *Chai* add up to eighteen."

"I have no idea what you're talking about," I said.

Talia laughed. "I guess you have to be Israeli to know about gematria. It's a Kabbalistic method of interpreting the Hebrew scriptures by computing the numerical value of words, based on those of their constituent letters."

I still wasn't sure what she was talking about, but I couldn't admit it. "Uh-huh ...so?"

"Well, Dr. Rose, it's a public secret that Department 18 of our government is an arm of our foreign intelligence service, Mossad, and it just so happens that Department 18 uses a *Chai* as its logo."

"So, you're implying the dental implant I have in my hand may have been produced by Department 18?"

"It's difficult to know. Let's just say stranger things have come out of that department."

I thanked Talia and gave her my cell phone number in case she came up with any more information. Then I hung up and just stared into space. What the hell was John Doe mixed up with?

Thirteen

Fog set in over the city, putting the kibosh on my weeklong tradition of cocktails on the deck; however, it didn't discourage me from creating a new concoction. I mixed Bloody Mary mix with horseradish, added a handful of ice cubes and finished it off with a celery stalk for garnish. I figured if I got fired from this job, I could always be a mixologist at a local non-alcoholic bar—if there actually was such a thing. Right on cue, my phone buzzed. I looked at the ID and let it go to voicemail.

One Virgin Mary is never enough. I poured another and went heavy on the horseradish. It felt like I had swallowed a red hot briquet from the barbecue and, as I made a dash for the ice cube tray, my phone buzzed again. This time it displayed a caller ID I didn't recognize and, normally, I wouldn't answer it, but this call had the same country code I had used for my morning inquiries—Israel. "Dr. Rose, here," I said.

"Dr. Rose, my name is Ari Levine. Would it be possible to have a few words?"

"About what?"

"It's rather sensitive. Perhaps we could meet for dinner. I'll explain."

The laws of probabilities told me it was no coincidence that the first time in my life I place a call to Israel, I would the same day get a call back from Israel. I had no intention of flying fourteen hours just to have dinner with this guy, so I said, "I doubt it. I'm in San Francisco."

The man laughed. "I think the country code may have thrown you off. My phone is from Israel, but I too am in San Francisco. I have an eight o'clock reservation at the Gary Danko restaurant. Will you join me?"

Levine knew how to get a person's attention. Gary Danko's was the most expensive restaurant in the city, and the wait for a reservation, even if you were well connected, was north of six months. "What's that restaurant's name again?" I asked.

"Danko ... Gary Danko. I hope to see you there at eight." Levine hung up.

The last time I had worn a suit was when Josie and I got married. I expected moths to fly out of the garment bag, but to my surprise the blue pinstripe was still pressed and in good condition. I was six feet, a hundred and seventy on our wedding day. I knew I hadn't shrunk and I'd only gained five pounds, so I figured it would fit. I still had the white shirt and silk navy tie that went with it, but the boutonniere had ended up in the trash—much like the marriage.

I decided to use the new Yellow Cab app and, to my surprise, the car showed up in less than five minutes. Ten minutes later, the driver dropped me off below Russian Hill on the corner of

Northpoint and Hyde. Considering how I was dressed; I felt the need to tip him five bucks.

Needless to say, I had never been to Gary Danko's. When I was in practice, I probably could have afforded the place, but on my new salary, I was happy I wouldn't be picking up the tab. I peered into the bar and was pretty sure I identified my host. A swarthy-skinned man in his middle fifties with gray hair and a well-trimmed goatee was looking at his phone while polishing off a martini. His dress was typical European: tight suit jacket, narrow pants and tapered shoes. "Mr. Levine?" I asked.

He turned, revealing a broad smile. "Dr. Rose, I'm so happy you decided to join me."

I wasn't sure if the conversation would be worth the trip, but I'd gladly trade an evening of boredom for a dinner at Danko's. "My pleasure," I said.

"What are you drinking?"

One would think this would be an easy question to answer. It wasn't. There I was in the fanciest restaurant in the city, dressed in a suit I'd only worn once, and in the company of a guy who looked like Sean Connery in his prime. "A Ritual Old Fashioned," I said. The bartender winked, indicating he could keep a secret. Ritual is a whiskey alternative—zero proof.

Levine pointed to his glass. "And Tony, another Cambridge Martini, please. You can send them to our table." Levine raised his finger and the maître d' seemed to appear out of thin air. He led us to a table with a gorgeous view of the bay and both bridges and positioned two menus in front of us.

"Have you been before?" Levine asked.

"No, first time."

"The Moroccan-style Spiced Squab is quite fantastic."

To me that sounded too much like a pigeon imported from Marrakesh. I ordered the seared beef filet. The elephant in the room was getting larger, so I decided not to pretend it wasn't there. "Okay Mr. Levine, why exactly are we here?"

"Please, call me Ari ...and may I call you Rick?"

I nodded and drained my artificial Old Fashioned.

"Rick, I believe you have been inquiring about Israel's Department 18," Ari said.

"Why would you think that?"

"That's not really important. Have you?"

"No."

"That's not what I heard."

The waiter placed the first course, a Dungeness crab salad, in front of me, but seafood didn't go real well with interrogation. "Well, maybe you heard wrong," I said.

"I doubt that."

"And who are you again?" I asked.

Apparently, the temperature level of the conversation was rising above the number Ari had anticipated. "Relax, Rick, I work for the Israeli consulate in Los Angeles."

I wasn't well schooled in politics or diplomacy, but in every mystery novel I ever read, the guy at the consulate was usually a spy. "Oh, yeah? What do you do there?" I asked.

"I'm kind of a PR guy. I take care of sensitive situations and smooth them over."

"So, I've gone from your dinner guest to a sensitive situation?"

"Rick, let's cut through, as you Americans say, the bullshit. You made a call this morning in which a woman name Talia introduced Department 18 into the conversation. Is that not true?"

I couldn't believe my ears. "So, did you tap my phone or Talia's? I never dreamed Israel would be spying on its own citizens."

"You don't understand, Rick. I know this is new to you, but it's so much more complicated than you think."

Ari may not have intended it to sound that way, but his tone reminded me of my dad when I asked him about the birds and the bees. I pushed away from the table just as the entrees arrived. "I understand enough."

Levine stood and put his arm on my shoulder. "Rick, please ...stay. We somehow got off on the wrong foot here, but I think we can help each other out. Besides, it would be a shame to waste that gorgeous beef."

I shoved his arm away. "No thanks," I said. "I'll stop at Arby's on my way home." I left Ari Levine with a plate of beef on the table and a nice helping of egg on his face.

Fourteen

Sleep didn't come easy for me that night. I took an Ambien, but my brain wouldn't turn off. I kept thinking that my first impression of Levine was probably correct. Department 18 is an arm of Mossad and Mossad is the equivalent of our CIA. Levine is most likely a spy. He knew I had called Talia, and he knew she told me about department 18, but he didn't know I was trying to identify John Doe ...or did he? Maybe I was too impulsive. Maybe I should have hung around. Maybe I could have learned a little more about Levine. Maybe Danko's had a great dessert menu. Maybe ...

The best part of being a recovering alcoholic is the absence of a hangover. I only got three hours' sleep, but I could function. Before going into the office, I stopped at a coffee truck that was parked outside our building. It was named Big Louie's Java, and Louie himself loaded me up with a healthy dose of caffeine and sugar. I felt good.

My secretary raised her head from the computer as I entered the office and it occurred to me that I said hello and goodbye every day, but knew nothing about her. "Good morning, Stella."

"Good morning, Dr. Rose. How was your evening?"

"Boring. How was yours?"

"Boring."

"Well, I guess at least we have the same interests," I said.

She laughed. "I guess we do. Oh, Dr. Rose, a gentleman from the Israeli embassy called. A mister ..."

"Levine."

"Yes, he asked for a return call ASAP."

I stepped into my office and took a deep breath. I knew I was going to have another meeting with Ari Levine, I just didn't know when. I lifted the phone, pushed three digits for the intercom and said, "Alex, it's Rick. Any chance we can talk?"

Alex asked that I give her ten minutes. I gave her twenty and knocked on her door. She motioned to an empty chair and handed me a cup of coffee. "Black with two sugars," she said. "What's up?"

I told her about my calls to Israel and about my meeting with Levine. "I think we may be getting in over our heads," I said.

"So, you think this guy is Mossad?"

"Pretty sure."

We sat in silence while Alex processed the information. After a few minutes, she said, "I really hate to call in the CIA. They're real pricks. They come in, throw their weight around, then disappear and leave us with a mess. First, let's see if we can get an identity for John Doe and try to figure out who Levine really is. How do you feel about setting up another meeting?"

I hesitated. My knowledge of the spy business was limited to three Jason Bourne movies, during two of which I'd fallen asleep.

"I'm fine with it," I said, as if I weren't questioning what the hell this job was getting me into.

"You don't seem fine."

"Just pissed at myself for walking away from a three-hundred-dollar dinner. What about Jim? Should we get the police involved?"

Alex wrinkled her nose. "Let's just keep this between the two of us."

The call-back number Levine had given to Stella used a U.S.A. area code. I googled it and Wikipedia popped up: *Area code 202 is the North American telephone area code for Washington, DC.*

I had a bad feeling about where John Doe was taking me, and it took a good half hour to muster the courage to dial Levine's number. When I finally did, to my disappointment, I received a recorded message. *"Ari Levine is unavailable. Please leave a short message."*

"Mr. Levine, uh, Ari, this is Rick Rose returning your call. You have my office and cell numbers. I'll be waiting for your call."

Out of the blue, a thought hit me. I tapped the intercom. "Dr. Reingold, here."

"Helmut, it's Rick."

"Oh, hello. What's up?"

"John Doe was wearing a tuxedo. Do you still have it?"

"For sure. We don't throw anything away."

"I'll be right down."

Helmut was relaxing at his desk when I walked in. He waved and pointed to a box on the floor next to him. "All his possessions."

There wasn't much, just the clothes he was wearing. I turned everything inside out looking for labels. The ones on his jacket, trousers, shirt and bowtie had been ripped off, but his assailant had missed John's boxer-briefs. The label read: Orlebar Brown, London. I placed everything back in the box and turned to Helmut. "Has anyone else looked at these?"

"Detective Allen checked the tuxedo and the shirt, but I don't think he looked at the under shorts."

"Good. Do me a favor and keep this just between us for now."

I headed back to my office and did a search for Orlebar Brown. It turns out he's a British clothes designer who uses the slogan: *Designed in London, made in Europe, worn across the World.* I made calls to Neiman Marcus, Saks and Nordstrom, asking if they carried this brand of underwear. I was told they did not. They were outlandishly expensive—sixty-five dollars apiece—and extremely difficult to find in the United States.

Just as I was getting ready to head home, my cell buzzed. I looked at the ID—area code 202. I decided to let it go to my voicemail greeting, *"This is Dr. Rose. Leave a message, and I'll get back to you."*

"Hello, Rick, it's Ari. I guess we're playing telephone tag. Get back to me when you can."

I turned off the lights, my computer, and my brain. I'd had enough for one day.

Fifteen

The body's homemade melatonin is the great equalizer. I woke up refreshed and ready to dive right back into the case. I thought it might be a nice gesture to bring a gift to Stella, but I didn't want it to look inappropriate, so I gently set a medium Frappuccino topped with whipped cream on her desk. When I got to know her better, I'd make it a large.

Her face lit up. "Oh, thank you, Dr. Rose. That's sweet of you."

"You're welcome ...and Stella ...call me Rick."

"Okay, sure ...Rick. By the way, I left a note on your desk. You had another call from Mr. Levine. Would you like me to get him on the line?"

I shook my head. "No, I'll do it myself. Thanks."

When I sat at my desk, Stella's memo was front and center. This time Ari had left a return number with a 213-area code. I recognized it from my UCLA days; it was for Los Angeles. I dialed the number, and it was answered on the first ring. "Levine, here."

"Ari, this is Rick Rose. My secretary said you had a doggie bag for me."

There was a pause before he responded. "Oh, I'm sorry about that. I left it for the waiter."

"Only kidding," I said. "So, still in the spy business?"

"Look, Rick, let's forget last night. Could we try again? I think you need me as much as I need you."

It occurred to me that he may be right, and I was probably wrong for walking out on him. "I'm guessing you blew your expense account at Danko's," I said. "Meet me at Tadich's around noon ...Dutch treat."

I was just about to head out for my lunch meeting when my desk phone rang. I had no idea who it was, so I answered the way I thought a professional should answer. "Dr. Rose."

An excited voice responded. "Rick, it's Helmut. I have a surprise for you. Guess what?"

"What?"

"Another John Doe checked in this morning with no identification and no prints on any local, state or federal registry."

I didn't respond, figuring more information would be forthcoming. Helmut didn't disappoint. "And guess what else?" he said.

Party games were never my long suit. "Helmut, this isn't twenty questions. Just tell me."

"Okay, okay. He's missing a lower second molar."

I was pretty sure Helmut's inference that John Doe #II was somehow related to John Doe #I was correct, but to make sure I asked, "Who made his underpants?" There was no response from the good doctor. "You still there?" I asked.

"Yes ...uh ...you actually want me to check his underpants?"

"Yes, if you would, please." I chuckled as I visualized Dr. Reingold pulling down the undies of his newest corpse.

After a two-minute pause, Helmut came back on the line. "Got it," he said.

"And?"

"They were made by a company named Orlebar Brown."

~ * ~

At one time in my life, I was a health nut; I spent an hour in the gym every day. But since the breakup, my primary exercise has been a trip or two to the bathroom, which I can't really say is on a daily basis. It was less than a mile from my office to the Tadich Grill, so I decided to get back in shape by walking.

Even flat walks are uphill in San Francisco, and I was exhausted when I stepped inside the restaurant, which was overflowing with yuppies from the financial district. I squeezed through the crowd and elbowed my way to the maître d'. He was the waiter who had served me on my last visit. Apparently, he had been promoted to 'host for a day.' Before I could even utter a word, he handed me a pen and a clipboard and said, "Hour wait. Put your name on the list."

I wrote down the name, Barack Obama, and began working my way to the back of the crowd, when I saw a head pop out of a booth and heard my name being called. It was Ari Levine; the sonofabitch had the best table in the joint.

"Good to see you again," he said as I slipped in across from him. "A little busy here today."

"Yeah, how did you get a booth?"

"The maître d' is a friend of mine."

"Really. I didn't think a guy like that would have any friends."

Ari laughed. "It's amazing how a couple twenties can buy a friend."

I knew I had said it was Dutch treat, but I had no intention of splitting the bribe with Ari. "Now, what're the chances of actually getting a waiter to the table?" I asked.

"I have another friend that will be right over."

This waiter turned out to have the same personality defect as the maître d'.

"Petrale sole," I said. "Heavy on the tartar sauce." He gave me a dirty look and scribbled something on a pad. As soon as he finished getting our order and headed back to the kitchen, without beating around the bush, I went straight to the point of our meeting. "So, how's the weather in Israel?"

"Have you ever been there?" Ari asked.

"No, but I received two Israel bonds for my bar mitzvah. Another twenty years, and I'll be able to cash them in."

"Well, if you ever make it over there, I want you to be my guest. I'll show you the whole country. It's fabulous."

"Thanks, maybe I'll take you up on the offer." I looked him straight in the eyes and said, "Why am I of interest to you, Ari?"

For most people a direct question of that sort would make them uncomfortable, but it slid off Ari's back like an ice cube on a hot day. "Why were you inquiring about Department 18?" he asked.

"That's not an answer, that's a question."

"Okay then. How about ...because you inquired about Department 18?"

"Look, Ari, I'm just a guy trying to make a living, working for the San Francisco Medical Examiner. I wouldn't know the difference between Department 18 and the lingerie department at Macy's."

He gave me a smile that conveyed a message of disbelief. "You sell yourself short, Rick. You're a licensed dentist in the state of California, who was hired by the medical examiner to help her identify bodies. I'm interested in one of those bodies, so that makes me interested in you."

"Oh, really? Which body is that?"

The meals arrived, and we tabled our conversation while we dug into the food. I stared down at my plate; the Petrale sole had come without any tartar sauce. I could swear the waiter was smiling when he left our table.

When we were finished, I asked Ari again, "Which body is that?"

"The well-dressed one."

"Was he one of your compatriots or one of your enemies?"

Ari hesitated a bit. "I ...I can't really say."

"That's interesting," I said. "Because I can't really say anything either. You told me over the phone that we might be of help to each other, but we're like a couple of predators who just keep stalking each other. I'll tell you what. You tell me who this guy is and I'll tell you what I found on him."

Ari nodded. "That sounds reasonable. I'll run it by my superiors."

"Great, and while you're at it, run a John Doe number two by them."

His eyebrows lifted almost to his hairline. "You found another body?" he said. I nodded. "Why do you think its related?" he asked.

"I have my ways." I got up from the table, dropped two twenties next to the butter dish and said, "By the way, what brand of undershorts do you wear?"

"What? I don't get it."

"Never mind," I said. "Call me after you talk to your boss."

Sixteen

I was getting tired of my unsuccessful dates with Ari Levine. When I was a young man, a restaurant rendezvous meant the relationship was moving in the right direction, and there was a nice reward waiting for me in the near future. I realize that pertained to romance, and this pertained to business, but how many times did I have to endure the company of someone I didn't particularly like before I got the metaphoric first kiss? I'd invested four hours and forty bucks into a relationship with Ari Levine and I still didn't know if this guy was wearing a black hat or a white one.

I decided I needed to clear my head, so I took a walk through the Soma district. It was once the city's skid row, but after urban renewal it turned into a high-priced condominium community, overflowing with chic restaurants and a couple of professional sports stadiums.

I'd forgotten that Oracle Park—the home of the San Francisco Giants—was only a couple of blocks away. Usually the games were sold out, but on a lark, I approached the will-call booth and was able to buy a re-sale ticket for thirty-two bucks. I can't remember now who they played, but I do remember they got blown out, 9-0.

After the game, I used my Uber app to arrange for a guy named Jake in a black BMW to meet me two blocks away on King Street. A head popped from the driver-side of a fairly new model, and a young, good-looking guy shouted at me from across the street. "Rick? I'm Jake." I waved and dodged a few cars to reach the BMW and jumped into the back seat. To my surprise, it was occupied by a guy who, maybe if compared to Mike Tyson, would be described as sort of good looking.

"Oh. Sorry," I said. "I thought this was my ride." I reached for the door handle, but the driver peeled rubber and the car took off. "Hey, gentlemen, you have the wrong guy. My parents wouldn't pay five bucks to get me back."

My ride sharing buddy said, "Shut the fuck up," and sank his fist into my stomach. I hadn't had the opportunity to inform him that I was a projectile vomiter and when he pulled his fist from my belly, I showered him with an order of Tadich's Petrale sole minus tartar sauce. He yelled to the driver, "Jesus H. Christ, he puked all over me."

The driver, who I assumed was not really named Jake, wasn't interested in his partner's problems. "Live with it," he said.

I really don't know why, maybe out of embarrassment, but I reached into my pocket and handed the guy a handkerchief. He didn't know what to say in response to an act of kindness, so he just grabbed it and wiped the front of his shirt.

The driver turned onto Market Street and headed west away from downtown. When the street narrowed and turned into a curvy, hilly drive, I was pretty sure where we were headed. Twin Peaks was one of the highest points in San Francisco—almost a thousand feet above sea level.

It was almost dinnertime when the BMW pulled into a remote parking spot at the far end of the visitors' lot. All the tourists had probably headed to the bars by then, because the lot was empty. The two guys pulled me out of the car and shoved me in the direction of a viewing platform. I hadn't been able to see Jake's face up close while he was driving, but now I had a full view. "You look familiar," I said. "Do I know you?"

Jake smacked me hard enough across the face to open a cut below my left eye. "You don't know me, and I don't know you." He pushed me forward. "Walk," he said.

I could feel a trickle of blood work its way down my cheek and I used my shirtsleeve to wipe it off. I shuffled toward the viewing platform. My vomit recipient pushed me up against a waist-high metal fence designed to keep viewers from falling down the steep incline. "What the hell do you guys want?" I asked. "I know it's not money."

"We want the crown you took off that corpse," Jake said.

"Crown? I don't have any crown."

The two guys looked at one another and, as if the scene were choreographed, each grabbed one of my ankles and hoisted me over the fence where I dangled with an upside-down, panoramic view of the city.

"Are you going to give us what we want or do we let go of your ankles?" Jake said.

I began to taste stomach juices work their way into my throat. "Yes, yes. I'll get it for you. I promise. Pull me back ...please."

The two thugs did what I asked and dropped me on the ground with a thud. Without another word, they turned, got into their car and drove off. When the sound of the car faded away, I stood and opened my phone, but I wasn't sure who to call. Uber was no longer on my favorites list, and I was embarrassed to call anyone at the office, especially Alex, so out of desperation I tapped in Josie's number.

Twenty minutes later, a red Prius pulled into the lot and dropped the driver's side window. I was face to face with my beautiful, crazy, ex-wife.

"Will you go with me?" she asked.

"Go? Go where?"

"You know where."

I was in no mood for *Jeopardy's* daily double. "No, I don't know and I don't want to know. Will you just drive me home, please?"

"I made an appointment with Dr. Rosenberg for next Friday. I'll take you home if you promise to go with me."

I read somewhere that torture victims will eventually agree to anything that's asked of them if it will stop the pain. I fell into that category and said, "Yes, I'll go with you." Josie opened the passenger door and I got in.

Seventeen

The next day I arrived late to the office. Earlier, when I looked into the mirror, I noticed my left eye was turning black. I ran to Walgreens and picked up some of that fake tanning cream and rubbed it under my eye. Unfortunately, when orange and black are mixed they make brown.

I put on a pair of large, horn-rimmed sunglasses and tried to shuffle by Stella while she was buried in her computer, but she was too sharp to deceive. "What happened to your eye?" she asked.

"Eye? What eye?" I asked.

"The brown one."

"Oh, that eye. I bumped into a door."

Stella tried to hold back a smile, but I could tell she was ready to break into a laugh. "A brown door, I assume," she said.

I hastened my pace to get away from her ridicule. "Yeah, watch out for those brown doors."

I'm not sure if Stella had given Alex a heads up or if Alex just happened to be in the vicinity, but an hour later she knocked on my door. I recognized the soft tap and, although I dreamt of having long conversations with Alex, this wasn't a good time. I raised my voice so it could be heard through the door and said, "I'm out of the office at this time. Check back later."

The door opened, and Alex stepped in. "Rick, what's wrong?" she asked.

"I'm thinking of quitting."

Alex frowned. "What? Why? You're doing such a good job."

"I'm beginning to think a long life beats $136,400 a year."

"I don't understand. What does one have to do with the other?"

"I've had a death threat."

"What? What kind of death threat?"

"Well, I think there's only one kind ...do what I say or I'll kill you."

Alex sat down in my spare chair and took a deep breath. "Who did this come from?"

"A couple messengers with big muscles."

"Messengers for who?"

"Don't know, but he wants John Doe's crown."

"... or they'll kill you?"

"That was the way I interpreted the message."

"I'm confused. How would they even know about the crown?"

I shrugged. "I have no idea. But just so you know, another body related to John Doe checked into the morgue yesterday."

"Why do you think they're related?"

I really didn't want to talk about teeth right now, and I didn't think this was the right time to lay out my underpants theory to the boss, so I said, "It's complicated, but take my word for it—they're related."

Alex stood and looked as though she were a lawyer pleading to the jury. "Rick, please don't quit. I'm going to get the police involved."

"I thought you said it was better to keep them out of this until we learned more."

"Just Jim Allen. He's an asshole, but a good cop. He'll keep it a secret while he looks into it."

After my last conversation with my homeless buddy, Gabe, I knew Jim Allen wasn't a good cop, and I was quite sure he couldn't care less about putting my life in jeopardy, but Alex was depending on me, and I didn't have the heart to let her down. "Okay," I said. "I'll hang around—for a while, anyway."

I decided to forego the stairs portion of my exercise program and rode the elevator down to the morgue. Helmut had apparently run out of cadavers to work on and was browsing through a six-inch-thick copy of Gray's Anatomy. He looked up when he heard the door buzz open. "Oh, hi, Rick," he said. "You ready to meet John Doe II?"

"Yeah, do I need to put on the scrubs and gloves?"

"No, just don't touch anything."

Helmut approached a refrigerated stainless-steel wall unit and slid out an ice-cold John Doe II. He was lying on his back, exposing a couple dozen stiches on his chest that Helmut had used to close up his surgery. They created an image of a giant cross where a twenty-inch vertical cut and a fourteen-inch horizontal incision intersected.

It was hard to look at and I casually averted my attention. "Find anything unusual?" I asked.

Helmut drew back my gaze when he pointed to the upper left abdomen. "There's a ruptured spleen in there ...probably hit with a baseball bat or something like that." He nodded toward John

II's head, which was cut open and swollen in a grotesque pattern. "That's the blow that killed him," he said.

I couldn't handle the gore any longer and nodded toward the personal property locker. "What was he wearing when he was brought in?"

"He was found in a homeless camp wearing a tee shirt and a pair of torn coveralls."

"You mean like workmen wear?"

"Exactly."

"You mentioned he was missing a lower molar ...like John I?"

"Looks that way to me." Helmut held up his palms. "But I didn't touch anything in the mouth. I left it for you."

I appreciated his confidence and his deference to me when it came to the oral exam, but to be honest, I wasn't that comfortable working on dead people. I guess I still knew more about the mouth than anyone else on the case so I said, "Great. That's great. Can you schedule me for tomorrow?"

Helmut took out a pocket size Day-Timer and jotted a note. "Nine a.m.," he said.

Eighteen

After my experience with the two goons in the BMW, Uber was definitely on my no-fly list. At the end of the day, I had Stella call for a cab, and I peeked into the back seat before getting in. It was a quiet ride home. The driver had earbuds in and was carrying on a conversation in Farsi with someone on his phone. When we reached my apartment house, he didn't bother to put the call on hold; he just kept talking as he sorted out change from my ten-dollar bill. I tipped him a generous two bucks and hustled to the front door.

I looked behind me and up and down the street for any suspicious activity. I wasn't sure what I would have done if there was any, but the street turned out to be empty, so it wasn't a problem. I tapped five digits on the building's security keyboard, and the door clicked open; I let out a sigh of relief and quickly stepped inside the lobby.

As I may have mentioned earlier, my unit was on the top

floor with a great view of the city. The only drawback was the two flights of stairs I had to negotiate to reach it. I was overheated and perspiring when I unlocked my door and stepped inside. The sweat instantly turned cold and clammy. The smell of cool salt air coming off the bay was refreshing to come home to, so I always made a habit of leaving the balcony slider open whenever I was gone. But today the apartment was warm and stuffy. I looked toward the balcony. The door was closed as tight as a drum.

I'd read enough Jack Reacher novels to know this was the time to get the hell out of there. I slammed the door and took two steps at a time toward the lobby. I could hear what sounded like a couple pair of boots hammering the wooden steps behind me. I threw open the entrance door and stepped onto the street. My hand was shaking so badly I could hardly tap the three numbers into my phone.

When my buddies from the Twin Peaks tour came rushing through the door and headed straight for me, I held up my cell, like a crucifix in front of a vampire, so they could see 911 on the display. They backed off and Jake said, "Get us what we want, Rose. You have twenty-four hours or the medical examiner will be looking for a new dentist to examine her corpses." They turned and sprinted off down the street.

I went back up to my apartment, but only long enough to pack a bag and call a cab. The driver opened the door for me, set my suitcase and laptop on the seat and asked, "Where to?"

I honestly didn't know, but I remembered my wedding reception had taken place in the garden court of the Palace Hotel, on the corner of Market and New Montgomery. I told the driver to drop me off at Second and Mission. After he pulled away, I lugged my suitcase and laptop a block west to New Montgomery and then headed north a half a block to the hotel's side entrance.

The Palace hadn't changed since my wedding. As a matter of fact, I was told it had hardly changed at all since it was rebuilt after the 1906 earthquake. When I stepped inside, I had a direct view of the familiar garden court. Waiters were flitting from table to table next to a marble dancefloor that was lit by a myriad of crystal chandeliers. A guy wearing a white jacket and a black bowtie saw me standing at the front desk and scurried over. He sort of lifted his nose in the air at the sight of me carrying my own luggage and asked, "Do you have a reservation?"

"Sir," I said.

He looked perplexed. "Sir? Sir, what?"

"Do you have a reservation ...sir," I said.

His nostrils flared. "Do you have a reservation ...sir?"

"Do I need one?"

"Uh ...no, we're half empty."

"Great. Give me the cheapest room you have."

He smirked as if he knew that request was coming and ran his finger down a computer screen. "I have a lovely room on the third floor facing Market Street?"

It was my turn to smile as if I knew that response was coming. "How about a quiet one on the tenth floor not facing the boulevard?"

We eventually agreed to an average one on the sixth level. When I was settled in, I double-locked the door and collapsed onto the antique bed. It was time to ask myself some tough questions regarding my new job, like: How the hell did I get here? What the hell am I doing here? Why the hell am I still here?

I knew how I got here. I needed the money and I was the only one who applied for the job. What I was doing here was a tougher question to answer. I had the title of forensic odontologist, but when I was honest with myself, I had to admit I didn't really know what that meant. I was doing my best to identify a couple of dead bodies, and I was obviously pissing some people off along the way.

Why I was still hanging around after two death threats was the result of a fantasy. I thought I could be the guy who rides in on a white horse and saves the damsel in distress—that damsel being Dr. Alexandra Keller. But then I had a reality check, which came with the sinking feeling that perhaps in the end it would be her riding in on the white horse to save me.

Only once in my life had I been in what I thought was love and that ended badly when Josie chose the cat over me. At this point in my life, I had to admit I didn't know what love really felt like. But when I was around Alex, it felt like how I thought love should feel. I answered my own question. I was still here because of Alex.

I don't know what came over me; I opened the mini-bar door. There they were, all my old buddies staring out at me—Jim Beam, Jack Daniels, Johnnie Walker and Jose Cuervo. I snatched a miniature of Jack and quickly closed the refrigerator door as if to trick my brain into thinking it had never been opened. There was a water glass in the bathroom. I tore off the sanitary lid and with one twist of the top, I opened the bottle and poured its amber liquid into the glass. I stared at it, and it stared back. I wanted to toss it down in one gulp, but then ...then the memories returned: lost license, lost practice, lost house, lost life. I dumped the booze into the toilet and flushed it.

I was wound up and couldn't slow my brain down. When I was finally able to doze off, I dreamt of a white horse. I wanted to see who was riding it, but every time I got close enough, something would distract me. The dream was exhausting, but eventually I was in position to make out the rider. I stretched my neck to get a look at the face and then ...woke with a start; it was six o'clock in the morning.

Nineteen

It was only a five-minute cab ride from the Palace to my office; just the right amount of time to ask myself how the goons knew I wasn't going to keep my promise. It had to be someone from the medical examiner's office. But who?

"Four bucks," the driver said.

I gave him a five and waved off the change. Even though it was only a little after eight, Stella was already at her desk when I walked into the office. "Morning, Rick," she said.

My brain went into turbo-paranoid mode. Was it her? Was Stella the mole? Wait a minute, I thought. This is a lovely young woman. What am I thinking? "Morning, Stella. Sorry, I didn't get us any coffee today."

She gave a little smile. "No, problem, you always bring it. I should take a turn."

"No, that's the boss's duty in this office. I'll bring you a tall one tomorrow. Anyone on the message machine?"

"Yeah, guess who?"

I didn't get many messages, so I figured it was either my ex-wife or Ari Levine. "I'll guess Levine."

Stella handed me a reminder note. "He wants to make another lunch date."

I shoved the paper in my pocket and waved to Stella as I disappeared into my office. As soon as I sat at my desk, the intercom buzzed. I tapped the red button. "Forget something?" I asked.

"No, Detective Allen is here to see you."

My initial thought was to keep him waiting for about a half hour, but my second thought told me that it might not be wise to piss off a cop who's been assigned to protect me. "Send him in," I said.

I was expecting Jim to come lumbering in like a bull in a china shop, but I was mistaken. He gave a gentle knock and opened the door just enough to peek his head inside. "Is this a good time?" he quietly asked.

"Come in, come in." I pointed to a chair facing my desk. "Sit down ...please."

Jim took a seat and adjusted his position just enough times for me to figure out he was uncomfortable. "Alex asked that we talk," he said.

"I know. Did she tell you about my chaperones?"

"Yeah, she did. You think that was a serious threat?"

I nodded. "Serious enough for them to break into my apartment yesterday."

Jim furrowed his brows. "They came at you again?"

"With vengeance. I slept in a hotel last night."

The detective stood and thrust his hand across the desk. "Rick, we got off to a shaky start and that was my fault. I apologize. How 'bout we start over?"

I'd never seen this side of Jim, and I wasn't about to miss out on an opportunity to mend the relationship. Hey, maybe Jim could be my best friend. I doubted it, but I held out my hand anyway, and we shook.

"What can of worms did you open?" he asked.

I didn't know what Alex had told Jim, but I was pretty sure it wasn't much. "I have no idea," I said.

Jim frowned. I knew he didn't believe me, but he let it go for now. "Listen, Rick, I'm going to put a man outside your building every night for a couple weeks," he grabbed one of my pens from the desk and jotted a set of numbers on a scrap of paper. "This is my cell ...use it night or day." He handed me the note.

I'd treated thousands of people when I was in practice, and I thought I was a pretty good judge of character. Was it possible I had misjudged Jim? I hoped so, but one polite meeting wasn't going to totally erase my initial opinion. "Thanks, Jim ...appreciate it," I said.

We walked to the elevator together and Jim bid me goodbye at the main floor. I continued on to the basement where John Doe II was waiting for his examination.

I had decided not to ask Alex to act as my assistant. It occurred to me that meeting over a dead body more than once could be detrimental to a serious relationship. I suited up and pulled the sheet off our cadaver. I almost lost my breakfast again when my eyes took in the facial damage and my nose took in the formaldehyde.

John II was a mess. I took x-rays and impressions of his teeth and then, except for the oral cavity, covered up what was left of his face. Charting the fillings in his teeth was easy; he had none. Exactly like John I, he had a perfect dentition except for a missing lower left molar, where an implant post—minus the crown—extruded through the gum.

A voice came from behind, and I think I jumped a foot. "You going to go after that implant?" Helmut asked.

"Oh, man, don't sneak up on me that way. This place is already spooky."

"Sorry, I didn't mean to startle you. So, why are you so interested in these implants, anyway? The crowns are gone."

It suddenly occurred to me that I really didn't know Helmut very well and, maybe, just maybe, he wasn't the right guy to confide in. For all I knew, he could be a spy from Transylvania. "I don't know, it's the only lead we have to these dead guys' identities."

"You want my help going after this one?"

I shook my head. "No, just dig up my bone saw and a few instruments, and I'll have it out in five minutes."

Helmut brought me a stainless-steel tray with sterilized instruments and a sterilized bone saw. I always wondered why examiners used sterilized instruments on dead people, but I didn't want to show off my ignorance, so I didn't ask. Helmut took a few steps back and watched the procedure. When I was done, I dropped the bone wedge containing the implant into a stainless bowl and handed it to him.

"I assume you want me to dissolve the bone off this, like I did the other one."

I laughed. "Not exactly. Don't overdo it this time. I need to read the manufacturer's name."

I cleaned up, dialed Alex's number and asked if she had the preliminary report on our new victim. She said she did and invited me to come to her office as soon as I was available. On the way up, I stopped to check with Stella. "Any new messages?"

"Ari Levine." She handed me a slip of paper. "Again."

"Thanks. Hey, Stella, if I dictate the report for today's procedure, could you get it out by tomorrow morning?"

"Sure, no problem. I got your last one out in less than hour."

Alex's secretary waved me toward the private office. I thought it proper to knock, but Alex called out before I was finished. "You don't have to knock. Come on in, Rick."

Alex's office was always a warm spot for me to land—probably because it was here that she had metaphorically saved my life by hiring me. "Coffee or tea?" she asked.

I was hoping for something a little more personal, but that's what fantasizing does to a guy. "Coffee ...two sugars," I said.

She poured two cups, and we sat silently for a minute until she said, "I heard Jim Allen met with you."

"Yeah, thanks for sending him over. I feel better now."

"So, you're not going to quit today?"

I smiled. "Not today."

Alex slid a manila folder across to me. "The prelim. An anonymous nine-one-one call sent the police to a homeless camp where they found our guy beaten to a pulp. He didn't have any identification, and his prints aren't on any local, state or federal registry."

I thumbed through the report, but skipped the colored photos. "I saw him in person this morning ...not a pretty sight."

"You said you thought this murder was related to the other one. Do you still think so?"

"I know so. Different wardrobe, but the same MO. His mouth was a carbon copy of John number one—no dental work except for a second molar implant with the crown removed."

Alex sighed. "Any thoughts on how we ID these guys?"

I chose once again not to mention my underpants theory, but I did tell Alex about Gabe, my homeless informant. "That's super work, Rick. Are you going to talk to him about John II?"

We were touching on a sensitive subject, one I felt uncomfortable broaching, but one that I knew had to be broached. I fidgeted around in my chair while Alex cocked her head and waited for me to say something. "Look, Alex, I promised this guy twenty-bucks every time he gives me something. Do I have some sort of expense account for this type of thing?"

"Of course. Give me a bill every time you pay him. We'll reimburse you."

"That's a relief. Say, while we're on the subject, I'm going to have to shell out some money while I court this Ari Levine guy. How big is this expense account?"

Alex flashed a big smile. "Rick, you're leading this investigation. Your budget is as big as you need it to be."

Twenty

I stopped by my office before calling it a day and, as usual, Stella was immersed in her computer. She looked up when I entered and handed me another message. This was a first for me—three messages in one day. "Do you know a woman named Joselle Freeman Rosenkofsky?" Stella asked.

"Josie? Oh, yeah, she's my Amway dealer. She gave me a free baggie of vitamin D and now that I'm hooked, she charges me a hundred bucks a hit."

Stella laughed. "Rick, you're so full of it. Anyway, your Amway dealer said 'don't forget the doctor appointment on Friday.'"

"Must be for rehab." I noticed Stella glance over and power off her computer. "Hey, what do you do on that thing all day?" I asked.

She turned pale and began to perspire, like I'd just caught her stealing government secrets. "Promise you won't tell?" she said.

I crossed my fingers. "Promise."

"I met a guy on a dating app."

"So, you communicate all day by computer?"

"Not all day, just for a few minutes. We went out on a date a few nights ago."

I really didn't mind if Stella had some 'me' time at work, and I didn't want to get involved in her personal life, but I did give her some fatherly advice. "Watch out. There's a lot of creeps out there."

"Oh, I know, I've dated a couple ... but Chris is different. He's really a good guy."

"Okay, but I'd suggest you don't use the office computer. People are watching."

"Really? Oh my God, are you sure?"

"No, not really, but I wouldn't take the chance." I stuffed the message into my pocket with the other ones and waved goodbye. "It's not worth getting caught."

I picked up my things from the Palace and took a cab to my apartment. I'm not sure what I expected—probably a squad car parked in front of the building—but I was disappointed. There was no police presence anywhere in sight. I figured someone was probably stationed in the lobby, but when I stepped inside, it was empty.

I searched my pockets and came up with the scrap of paper with Jim's cell phone number. I tapped it into my phone and he answered on the third ring. "Detective Allen, here."

"Jim, it's me, Rick."

"Yeah, Rick, what's up?"

"I'm in my building, but I'm afraid to go up to my apartment. Where's your guy?"

"Guy? What guy?"

"You said I'd have protection."

"Oh, yeah, sorry. Got involved in something and forgot. Sit tight, I'll be right over."

Needless to say, the confidence I had placed in Jim Allen this morning was waning. I sat on the curb in front of my building for fifty-eight minutes before I saw a black Ford Taurus round the corner and screech to a stop six feet from where I was sitting. Jim hopped out and gave me a thumbs up. "I'm here," he said in a tone that sounded as if he expected a trophy for participation.

I got up off the curb. "Yeah, so am I."

I didn't know if Jim had the sensitivity to realize I was pissed, but if he did, he ignored it. He just smiled and said, "Let's go upstairs."

My apartment door was ajar. Jim pushed me aside and unholstered his service revolver. He stepped inside using both hands to hold his pistol in front of him. After sweeping the room with his weapon, and when he was convinced no one was in the apartment, he waved me in.

A surge of nausea swept over me. Everything in my place had been upended. The furniture in the living room was overturned, the desk drawers had been emptied onto the floor and the papers burned. The kitchen was torn apart; all the dishes were on the floor smashed into a million pieces. However, my bedroom was intact except for a rope that was tied into a hangman's noose and laid at the foot of my bed.

"Well, they certainly sent a message. Why?" Jim asked.

"I promised I'd give them something ...but I didn't."

"What?"

"Something from one of the bodies."

Jim looked puzzled. "I don't get it," he said.

"Yeah, I don't either, but I think somebody's afraid I'm getting too friendly with the John Doe brothers."

"How would they even know about them?"

"I was going to ask you that."

Jim's eyes turned to steel. "Are you saying I leaked something?"

I realized I had gone too far and tried to walk it back. "Hey, Jim, I'm just putting you on."

"Yeah? Well, it's not funny. You can take care of yourself ...don't bother to call me again." He walked out and left me staring at the noose on my bed.

Twenty-one

I glanced at my watch; it was a little after six. I used my phone to Google *locksmiths near me.* The first to pop up was A1 Locks with an advertisement that read, *anytime day or night.*

I dialed the number and a guy who sounded like he was talking over happy hour noise at the local bar answered with the cordial greeting, "Yeah, what d'ya want?"

"Is this A1 Lock?" I asked.

"Oh, yeah, sorry, I thought you were my wife. What can I do for ya?"

"I need a new, heavy-duty lock."

"Okay, give me your address. I'll come by tomorrow."

"No," I said. "I need it now."

"I'm a little busy right ..."

"Your website said, anytime day or night."

There was silence on the other end of the phone. Finally, the guy said, "Two-hundred bucks plus parts, and I'll be there in a couple hours."

"How about three-hundred cash plus parts, and you be here in twenty minutes?" I guess I hit the magic numbers, because he took my address and showed up in a half hour.

It was after nine by the time Mr. A1 handed me the keys to my new lock. It was huge, it was brass, and it was expensive. Luckily, I had pulled seven-hundred from the ATM around the corner before he arrived.

I wasn't sure how to make contact with Gabe, but I knew where his favorite alley was, and I headed for it. I could smell the garlic coming from the Stinking Rose a block away. When I went around to the back, Gabe wasn't there. I roamed behind other nearby restaurants and asked the alley residents if they'd seen him. Most were afraid to respond, but one guy who looked to be an octogenarian sporting a gray, waist-length beard motioned me to follow him. He led me to the City Lights bookstore, an old fifties and sixties beat generation hangout on Columbus Avenue. The old man never spoke, just pointed inside. I handed him a twenty, which I would be sure to charge to my unlimited expense account.

The sign on the front door read: *open until 10 p.m.* I looked at my watch, it was 9:53. I stepped inside and immediately spotted Gabe in the far corner with his head buried in a book. He didn't look up as I approached, but when I was six feet away, he said, "Hey, Rick, what's doing?"

"How about dinner ...on me," I said.

He took out a pocketful of torn scraps of paper and began piecing them together like a jigsaw puzzle. "Let me check my schedule." When they were arranged to his satisfaction, he said, "Yeah, looks like I'm free tonight."

I had no idea when Gabe last had a genuine sit-down restaurant meal. I knew the famous North Beach Restaurant was only a block away, so we packed up Gabe's shopping cart and headed down Columbus.

The *maître d'* took one look at Gabe's attire and said the kitchen was closed. I knew that was bullshit because a waiter just passed us with a tray of pasta Bolognese and an order of Sand Dabs. I had a hundred-dollar bill left over from my trip to the ATM, and I held it in front of the guy's face. "You can take this and give us a table or I can ask for your boss and give it to him instead. Either way, we're eating here tonight."

The guy snatched the bill and led us to a table in the far corner of the dining room; it suited us just fine. He handed each of us a menu, "Is there anything else I can do for you?" he asked.

I made direct eye contact with this jerk. "Yeah, you can kiss my ass."

Gabe was still laughing when the cocktail waitress approached to take our drink orders. I turned to him, "I don't do well with alcohol, but you're welcome to order one if you'd like."

Gabe held up his hand. "I'm an AA alum—all twelve steps. Water's fine."

At that moment, I realized I knew nothing about this man with whom I was about to share a meal. "What was your previous life like, Gabe?" I asked. He stared down at the table, and I knew I was sending him to a painful place. I regretted asking. "Hey, it's none of my business. Let's order dinner," I said.

He held up his hand. "No, it's all right. You're the first person who even recognized I had a previous life. He paused, took a slug of water and let out a big breath. "I grew up in a foster home and on my eighteenth birthday, I was outta there." He took another gulp of water. "I got a job for minimum wage at the In-N-Out Burger on Jefferson Street and, in two months, I worked my way up to assistant french fry manager. It paid another two bits an hour, and I was able to rent a room in the Outer Mission district for twenty bucks a week."

I was so engrossed listening to Gabe's story that I didn't see the waiter standing impatiently next to our table. He cleared his throat a couple times. "Oh, sorry," I said. I knew Gabe would feel uncomfortable ordering an expensive dinner on my credit card, so I ordered for both of us. It was common knowledge that the North Beach Restaurant was one of the best Italian eateries in the city and I went for it—a starter of fried calamari, a couple Caesar salads and two entrees of risotto pescatore.

I didn't push Gabe. I figured he would continue his story when he was ready. We made small talk through the calamari and the salad. When the entrées arrived, the risotto was so outstanding neither of us spoke as we devoured it.

Gabe finished off his dish and patted his lips with his napkin. "Do you really want to hear more?"

I nodded. "I do. I really do."

"Okay, where was I? Oh, yeah. So, I knew frying potatoes wasn't going to be my career job, but it was paying the rent, plus I got a twenty-percent discount on my food. I decided to hang onto the job and keep my eyes open until an opportunity, any opportunity, came my way." He paused and swallowed hard before continuing. "A couple months later ..." His voice cracked and he paused again. "A couple months later ...a couple ..." A faraway look swept over his face—kind of like the one I had when my mom told me they were putting the dog down. "Do ...do you mind if we talk about this some other time?"

"No, of course not," I said.

A tear formed in the corner of his eye and he wiped it away with his finger. "Why were you searching North Beach for me?"

"Another body showed up yesterday."

"So why search me out?"

"The guy was found dead in a homeless camp under the 101 freeway. I thought maybe there was ...like a homeless network ...or something like that ...and I thought maybe you could get me some information about him." I suddenly felt pretty stupid and pretty condescending.

"What kind of information?"

"How he got there. Who he talked to. Maybe even who killed him."

Gabe's demeanor turned cold. "I'll see what I can find out."

Twenty-two

I slept well, knowing that a lock designed for Fort Knox was protecting my front door. I didn't want to disappoint Stella two days in a row, so on my way into the office I picked up two large, hazelnut, vanilla lattes from Big Louie's truck that, as usual, was parked right outside the building.

"Surprise," I said.

Stella's eyes lit up. "Wow, a latte. Did I do something good, or did you do something bad?"

"I owed you one. Any messages?"

Stella rolled her eyes. "Him again. When are you going to call him back?"

I winked at her. "It looks like Ari Levine wants to talk to me more than I want to talk to him. So, the longer I wait, the more eager he'll be when I do decide to call him."

"I'm impressed," Stella said. "Did you learn that from a psychology class at UCLA?"

"No, I learned it from my first girlfriend who said she'd call me back but never did."

I tossed Ari's message in the pile with his others. He could wait. My first order of business was to touch base with Helmut and rather than call him, I decided to head down to the morgue.

When the elevator door slid open in the basement, so did my olfactory receptors; it made me want to bring up Louie's hazelnut, vanilla latte. "I hate this smell," I muttered.

As usual, when I entered the morgue, Helmut was doing surgery on a corpse using sterilization protocol. He could have convinced me he was doing open heart surgery if I didn't know better. I raised my voice to be heard above what I recognized as a Chopin nocturne, which was streaming from his phone into the ceiling speakers. "Hey, Doc, got a minute?"

Helmut looked up. "What?"

I pressed pause on his phone. "Can we look at that implant?"

"Oh, sure," he said, as he stripped off his mask and gloves.

I followed him to the microscope table where he turned on his precious ten-thousand-dollar Zeiss Discovery.V8 Stereo. He slid the implant onto the viewing stage and I looked through the eyepiece. "A Chai," I said. "The same Hebrew letters as the other implant." Helmut nodded and smiled.

Once formaldehyde permeates fabric, the odor doesn't go away. When I returned to my office, I could still smell the morgue on my clothes. I hit the intercom and Stella answered. "What's that sweet smelling perfume you wear all the time?" I asked.

"It's called White Shoulders and it's not perfume."

"What is it then?"

"It's cologne. The perfume costs a fortune."

"I see. Could I borrow a few drops?"

There was a pregnant pause over the intercom. "You want to use my cologne?"

"Please, if you don't mind."

Ari Levine had several different phone numbers; I decided to use the one with the L.A. area code. It went to voicemail, but in the middle of the message it was interrupted by an actual voice. "Rick? Ari. I've been waiting for your call."

"Okay, what's up?" I asked.

"We have to meet."

"Ari, I'm tired of meeting with you, tired of having meals with you, and frankly I'm plain tired of you."

"Look, Rick, I'm sorry about the past, but I've been given permission to share information with you."

I knew Alex had given me the green light to spend money on this guy, but I wasn't going to sit through another pompous restaurant display, so I said, "I'm not available for lunch or dinner. How about you stop by my office?" There was no response. "You still there?" I asked.

"Yes, yes, I'm here. I'm afraid I can't do that."

"Really? Why's that?"

"In my business, I try to keep my face off security cameras. How about we just meet after work for a drink?"

"You're becoming a pain in the ass, Ari. Do you know a guy named Jake?"

"Jake? No, why?"

"Just a hunch. Okay, I'll meet you for a drink." There was an upscale bar in Chinatown that I knew served non-alcoholic drinks on request. "Do you know where the Asian Speakeasy Lounge is?"

He laughed. "Are you serious?"

"Yeah, meet me there at six."

"I don't know where it is."

"Google it. Six, sharp." I hung up.

Twenty-three

I walked to the foot of California Street and jumped on a cable car that was headed toward the top of Nob Hill. Instead of hanging off the side like most of the tourists, I sat down next to the gripman. With one hand, he was pulling a rope to play a tune with his bell and with the other he was manipulating a waist high lever to engage and disengage the constantly moving cable. "Ya headed up to the Fairmont hotel?" he asked.

"No, just Grant Avenue," I said. "Give it an extra ring when we get there. Will ya?"

"No problem, man." He went back to his bell and continued his serenade.

About six or seven blocks later, the tune was interrupted with a *clang, clang*. I gave the guy a thumbs up, and I hopped off in the middle of Chinatown.

The Asian Speakeasy Lounge was only a half a block away. I looked at my watch. It was almost six-thirty and I figured by now Ari would be on his second drink and getting impatient—perfect.

When I stepped inside the bar, a trio was in one corner playing blues music, and Ari was in another, sitting at a table away from the happy hour crowd. He waved two fingers in the air when he saw me come in, and I joined him at the table. "I see you found the place," I said.

"Yes, this 1930's motif is very ...how do you say it in America? Very ...cool."

An exotic-looking gal in a low-cut top, short skirt and high heels approached and set a paper doily on the table. She smiled in my direction. "Something to drink?" she asked.

"A Ritual Old Fashioned, if you have it?"

"You ordered that at Danko's," Ari said. "I've never heard of Ritual whiskey."

I'd been drinking this American made, zero proof whisky substitute ever since my graduation from the diversion program, but I wasn't about to tell Ari that, so I said, "It's a well-kept secret. They make it in Scotland and only produce eight-hundred barrels a year. You should try it sometime."

"I'll do that," he said.

I noticed Ari was raising his nose and sniffing the air. "What?" I asked.

"Are you wearing perfume ...White Shoulders maybe? I used to date a woman that smelled like you."

"It's cologne—not as expensive as perfume." I knew he was wondering why I was wearing a women's cologne, but I felt no obligation to explain. Just then, my drink arrived, and I pushed it in Ari's direction. "Want a taste?"

He forced a smile. "Maybe next round."

I took a slug of my cocktail and winced, like I would if actual alcohol was burning its way down my throat. "Okay, buddy, why are we here?"

"First of all, I work for the Israeli Mossad."

"Tell me something I don't know?"

An edge of a smile appeared on Ari's face. "So did your two John Does."

"And why are you sharing this with me?"

"I've done my research. You're the only guy who does the oral examinations in the medical examiner's office."

"So?"

"So, I believe you're in possession of two gold crowns which my organization wants back."

My mind was racing. I had the implants with the Hebrew lettering, but I didn't have the crowns. Ari Levine, however, was convinced I did. "What about your comrades? Don't you want them back?" I asked.

"Of course I would like them back, but in my business, business comes before sentiment. I want those crowns."

"Why?"

"That, Rick, is none of your concern, but we're willing to make a deal. Give us the crowns and we'll give you the dead men's birth certificates. We get what we want, and you get what you want."

Once upon a time, I read that 'truth is often harder to believe than fiction,' so I thought I'd give it a try. "I don't have them," I said.

Ari's eyes narrowed. "I don't believe you."

I couldn't remember who wrote that bit of wisdom, but the guy must have been a genius. "Well, it's true," I said.

"If you don't have them, I'm sure you have access to them. It would be a personal favor to me ...please ...get me the crowns."

I smirked. This guy wasn't my friend, and he wasn't qualified to ask me for anything personal. "You call me a liar, and now you want a favor? Well, in my business, business also comes before sentiment."

Ari's demeanor changed. "I'm authorized to give you a hundred-thousand ...cash."

My head began to spin. I knew I was getting in deep, but this was more than I had bargained for—way above my paygrade and way below my comfort level. "Is this a ...a bribe?" I asked.

"Let's just say it's a gift ...and let's make it two-fifty."

I didn't need a master's degree in deductive reasoning to realize I was dealing with some serious shit here; stuff that, if I was right, could get me killed. I suddenly had the urge to get the hell outta there. "I'll think about it," I said.

Ari stood and tossed the remainder of his drink down his throat. "Don't think too long or it might be too late."

"Too late? Too late for what?" As soon as those words came out of mouth, I regretted saying them.

He set his glass on the table along with a twenty. "Too late for you, my friend."

Twenty-four

The next day, I spent twenty minutes in my think tank—a stall shower with a three-way head that delivered oscillating hot water against my stiff neck—while I tried to make sense out of the predicament I had gotten myself into.

Yesterday, I had received my third death threat in as many days. Two from a couple of thugs who were certainly doing someone else's bidding, and the other from a spy for the Israeli Mossad. It was pretty obvious I was close to something that was worth killing for, and that something was a couple of gold crowns taken from my John Does. But I didn't have those crowns. Then, like a baseball bat smacking me between the eyes, the epiphany hit me. As long as my nemeses believed I had the crowns, I was safe. No one would kill the king without first getting the keys to the kingdom.

I went to the office that morning with a sense of power. I felt what Superman must have felt before the discovery of Kryptonite. As usual, Stella was at her desk when I walked in. I reached in my paper bag and took out a mocha with an extra squirt of chocolate. "Just for you," I said, as I set it in front of her.

"Geez, Rick, you're going to spoil me."

"I doubt it. Say, how's it going with the guy from the dating app?"

Stella blushed. "Good, really good."

I raised my eyebrows. "Sounds like it's past the kissing stage."

Stella's face turned a deeper shade of red. "Come on, Rick, you're embarrassing me."

"Okay, sorry. Hope it works out for you."

I stepped into my private office, and in an instant, my feeling of omnipotence disappeared as my sympathetic nervous system began pouring adrenalin into my arteries. My desk drawers had been ripped from their slots and thrown against the walls. My papers were strewn all over the floor, and my desk computer had been smashed with a paperweight that was still lodged in its screen. What most unnerved me though, was the Kryptonite that hung from the corner ceiling—a hangman's rope with my business card wedged into its knot.

Before I could recover from the shock, the intercom, which was on the floor somewhere, buzzed. I heard Stella say, "Detective Allen is here to see you."

I opened the door and made eye contact with Jim. "I thought you were pissed at me," I said.

"I got over it."

I motioned him inside where he took in the vandalized scene. "Whoa, when did this happen?"

"Last night, I guess, but how could they get by the alarm?"

Jim began taking pictures with his phone and, when he was satisfied he had enough of them, he yanked down the rope. "They must have had a key."

"A key ...to the building ...to my office? That's impossible."

Then, Jim surprised me. A guy who I figured never read a book in his entire adult life quoted a famous line from a Sherlock Holmes novel. *"Once you eliminate the impossible, whatever remains, no matter how improbable, must be the truth."*

Wow, I was impressed. "That's what you're going to do?" I asked.

"That's what detectives like me are taught to do."

I realized then that I had given Jim too much credit. He most likely memorized the quote from a detective instruction manual. "So, why did you come here this morning?"

Jim scrolled through the pictures on his phone and held one up so I could see it. "Ya know this guy? He dropped your name to me."

It was a horrible photo of Gabe, but he was recognizable. "Uh-huh, I know him. Why the picture?"

"I picked him up rummaging through a crime scene."

I knew right away which crime scene, but I asked anyway. "What crime scene?"

"Your second John Doe's."

It was heartwarming to know that Gabe had gone right to work on his assignment, but it was problematic for me, as I didn't want Jim to know Gabe was there at my behest. "He's a derelict I give a few bucks to on my way to work," I said.

I could see Jim was trying to put Sherlock's 'impossible theory' to use, but it wasn't equating properly for him. "Why would you give a bum your name?" he asked.

"I gave him my card ...I give everyone my card ...hey, did I ever give you one?"

He slipped the card from the hangman knot. "No ...I'll keep this one, thanks. I think your derelict guy may know something. I'm going to loosen him up in a cell for a few days."

I'd never taken lessons, but I knew I'd better start tap dancing. "Give the poor bastard a break. He's homeless and probably has his stuff in a shopping cart somewhere. In a few days, it'll vanish."

"So, what do you care?"

"My brother was in the same boat once."

"Oh, yeah? Where's your brother now?"

"He's dead. A cop shot him."

Jim wasn't sure what to make of that statement, but he knew if I was telling the truth, he'd better drop the subject. He chewed on his lower lip for a few seconds, then said, "Okay, I'll let the guy go."

I nodded, knowing my brother was actually in Baltimore, teaching the genome theory of genetics to third year students at Johns Hopkins School of Medicine.

Twenty-five

I spent the rest of the day thinking about Ari Levine's bribe offer; not because I was considering taking it, but because of what might happen to me if I didn't.

When I got back to my apartment that evening, I made myself a Tequila Sunrise, *sans* the tequila—four parts orange juice, one part lime juice, one part grenadine—and while I sipped the concoction, I once again thought about Ari's offer. Without inviting it, I was getting involved in some sort of espionage plot. A spy had offered me money and threatened my life if I didn't take it.

Something didn't equate. Why would an Israeli spy bribe me, threaten me, and not give a shit about his own dead comrades? Everything I'd ever read about the Mossad contradicted that scenario. Maybe, I thought, Ari Levine was a rogue spy and maybe he wasn't following Mossad protocol.

Looking back on what I did next makes me cringe from my naiveté. I googled the time difference; Tel Aviv was ten hours ahead of San Francisco. I figured if I called at eleven p.m. my time, I'd catch an agent in Tel Aviv at nine in the morning. It sounded like a good plan. I'd just ask him if everything Ari Levine was doing was on the up and up.

A computerized voice answered initially in Hebrew, but then began reciting the greeting in several other languages. When the recording rolled over to English, I tapped the 'O' key. A woman's voice came on the line. "This is the Mossad answer line, how may I direct your call?"

My mouth suddenly felt like I had just chewed a wad of cotton. I took a quick swig of water and said, "Uh, I'm calling from the U.S.A. Could I speak with an agent?"

"What is the nature of your call?"

I thought that was a very strange question, considering I was talking to a spy agency. "It's quite confidential," I said.

"Please hold for Field Agent Katz."

There was a click and, to my surprise, Simon and Garfunkel began serenading me with the second verse of Bleecker Street. The line clicked again and a deep male voice came on. "Dovid Katz ...what can I do for you?"

The cotton that I had just spit out filled my mouth again and my voice jumped an octave and a half. "I'm ...I ...I represent the medical examiner of the City and County of San Francisco. I've been working with one of your agents here."

"And your name, sir?"

"Oh, yeah, sure. I'm Dr. Richard Rose, forensic odontologist for the examiner."

"Okay, Dr. Rose, what brings your call this morning?"

I was tongue-tied. I hadn't rehearsed what to say and now I felt stupid for even having made the call. A few words managed to dribble out. "I, uh, want to talk to you about Agent ...uh, Ari Levine."

I sensed a slight hint of condescension in Dovid Katz's voice. "Surely, Dr Rose, you understand I can't talk to a stranger about any of our agents or our operations and if I did, it wouldn't be over the phone."

"Oh ...yeah, sure, I understand. How would I go about breaking through that barrier?"

"I suggest you come into our Tel Aviv office and meet with me."

"But ...but I'm in the U.S."

"I know where you are, Doctor, but if you wish to talk to us about an operative, you must either come to Israel or go through proper channels with your Central Intelligence Agency in Washington, D.C."

Oh, man, I thought, now the CIA will get into this and that's exactly what Alex didn't want to happen. "So, if I do come over there, what's the protocol?"

Katz cleared his throat. "You bring your superior with you and we talk."

"You mean the medical examiner?"

"That's correct ...and bring credentials for both of you."

"I get it. Will you be our contact?"

"I will. Use this extension when you call to set the appointment ...6232."

I thanked agent Dovid Katz and hung up. "What an ass I made of myself," I muttered.

I only managed a few minutes of sleep that night; questions about Ari Levine kept popping into my head. Maybe Katz was actually Levine's boss. Maybe Katz was luring me to Israel to hold me hostage for those crowns. Maybe Katz had informed the CIA about me. Maybe, just maybe, my imagination was getting the best of me.

I knew the time had come for a heart to heart with Alex. I arrived early to my office and stationed myself in front of my corner window, where I could see everyone arriving for work. At eight forty-five, Alex emerged from the parking garage and headed for the building's entrance. She was wearing a navy-blue pants suit, a white blouse and low heels. As usual, she looked magnificent—professional and yet sexy.

I figured she would be in her office in five minutes, but I gave her around fifteen before I tapped on her door. I would have loved to be greeted with a hug or maybe a peck on the cheek but instead, I received a smile and a handshake—so much for great expectations. "So, I assume you're here bright and early to give me news on our guests in the morgue," Alex said.

I let it all out. I told her about Jake and his buddy breaking into my apartment; I told her about both John Does having the same underwear; I told her about the demand and death threat from Ari Levine; I told her about Jim arresting Gabe. Yes, I told her everything, except what I really had come to tell her.

Alex inhaled like a swimmer coming up for air. "Whew," she said. "That's a lot to take in all at once. How are you holding up? Are you good seeing this through?" she asked. I wasn't sure what 'seeing this through' really meant, but I nodded in the affirmative. "Great, then what's our next step?" she asked.

The time had come to drop it on her. "Alex, I need you to go to Tel Aviv with me."

At first, she thought I was joking. "Why not Paris?" she said.

"I'd love that, but that would be for pleasure. This is for business."

Her smile disappeared. "You're serious?"

"Very," I said. "If you want me to get to the bottom of all this, I have to know if Ari Levine is acting on his own or with the blessing of the Mossad. I talked to Tel Aviv, and they told me if I wanted any information, to show up there with my boss and our credentials."

"What's plan B?" Alex asked.

"Call the CIA and turn everything over to them."

Alex winced. "I really don't want to go there," she said. "As I mentioned, I did it once, and they took over our entire office. It was a good year before we were whole again."

I had already done the math, and I laid it out for her. "Okay, here's how it would work. El Al has a direct flight at eight-fifteen every morning. It's about a fourteen-hour flight with a ten-hour time change, so we'd get there the next day around nine a.m. We get our answers, spend one night at a hotel and fly back the following day—elapsed time, three days."

"When would we leave?"

"The sooner the better ...tomorrow, if I can confirm the meeting."

Alex stepped to her desk and ran a finger over her calendar, while I held my breath in anticipation. A thought popped into my head that maybe I was more interested in taking a trip with Alex than I was in getting answers to this puzzle. I quickly let go of that notion when she turned and slid her desk phone in my direction. "Confirm it," she said.

Twenty-six

I looked at my watch. It was nine-twenty a.m.—seven-twenty p.m. in Tel Aviv. My stereotypical image of a spy placed Dovid Katz in a bar somewhere, drinking martinis that were 'shaken not stirred,' but on the chance I was wrong, I figured I'd give him a call. I punched the Mossad phone number into my cell and, as soon as I got the recorded message, I tapped in extension 6232. To my surprise a human voice answered. "Katz," it said.

In my haste, I had forgotten to clear my throat before I dialed, so when I responded it sounded like a piece of lettuce was caught in my windpipe. "Agent Kass ...Katz. This is Rick Rose from San Francisco."

"Yes, of course. What can I do for you, Dr. Rose?"

"How's Friday for our meeting?"

"What time?"

"Our plane gets in around nine in the morning. How's eleven o'clock?"

"Are you bringing your superior?"
"Yes, Dr. Alex Keller."
"Fine, I'll leave your names with the security detail."

I started to thank him, but he had hung up. I asked Stella to arrange the plane tickets and hotel reservations in Tel Aviv, and then I agreed to meet Alex at the SFO international terminal at six the next morning.

Jim had run Gabe through the ringer, and I was worried Gabe was lying low, and I wouldn't be able to find him. I searched the restaurant alleys, the City Lights bookstore and Washington Park, the nearest one to North Beach—all with no luck. Then it occurred to me that Jim arrested Gabe in the underpass near the 101 freeway, where the second body was found. I hailed a cab.

The smell of urine and feces that permeated the air around the encampment made me want to puke. Makeshift tents staked out personal space for about twenty residents whose meager belongings were strewn along the dirt bordering the on-ramp entrance to the freeway.

As I made my way from one plot to the next, the occupants eyed me with a combination of fear and anger. When I asked if anyone had seen a guy fitting Gabe's description, most of the squatters retreated into their tents. The others replied with a middle finger and a "fuck you" or an "up yours."

As I neared the end of the village, I spied a man sleeping on two pieces of torn cardboard. It was him. It was Gabe. When I approached, he opened one eye; the other was purple and swollen shut. His voice was weak, but he managed to whisper, "H ...hi ...R ...Rick."

I kneeled and cradled his head in my hands. "Did the detective do this to you?" I asked. Gabe just stared off in space. "Can you walk?" He nodded, and I helped him to his feet. "I'm taking you to my place. Where's your stuff?"

"It's g ...gone."

I helped him to a nearby side street and called a cab; when it arrived, the driver took one look at Gabe and was hesitant to let us in. I pulled a twenty from my wallet and handed it to him. "Trust me," I said.

I had the driver drop us in the back of my apartment building where there was a small elevator that was used by the service people. When I got Gabe inside my apartment, I sat him down on the couch, stepped inside the bathroom, and began running warm water into the tub. I returned to the living room and looked at Gabe's right eye. The skin above the brow was split and oozing blood. "Let me put a Steri-Strip on that," I said.

"Leave it. It's fine."

"It'll leave a nasty scar."

Gabe began to laugh. "Like I give a shit."

I handed him a towel, a set of clothes and some shoes from my closet, then pointed him toward the bathroom. "Take as long as you like," I said.

It's amazing what the absence of dirt and the addition of clean clothes can make on a man's appearance. Except for the eye, Gabe looked like a regular eight-to-five working guy. In addition to his appearance, his demeanor had also changed. The slouch he exhibited earlier had disappeared, and he stood upright like a confident man; as I could have predicted, his recurrent stutter had disappeared. "Thanks, Rick. Thanks a lot," he said.

"No need. If I hadn't asked you to nose around, you wouldn't have gotten beaten up."

"Rick, I talked to a guy who was there the other night. He saw them drop the body. It was just like what I saw behind the restaurant, except no dumpster."

"What did he say?"

"He described the same car—a big, black, Mercedes SUV with the insignia GLS 600. He said they just opened the back door and shoved him out."

I didn't keep a lot of food in the house; without a wife or a cat, there didn't seem much need. I was, however, able to throw together a couple of PB & J's on whole wheat toast—my favorite when I was growing up in Brooklyn.

We sat at the table eating our gourmet lunch and to my surprise, Gabe seemed to enjoy it more than he had our dinner at the North Beach Restaurant. "Anything else I should know?" I asked.

Gabe's face showed a troubled expression, one that looked like he wanted to tell me something, but all that came out was, "Uh, no. Uh ...nothing I can think of."

"You sure?"

"Yeah, I'm sure. Rick ...why? Why do you care so much about who dumped the bodies? You're a doctor, not a cop."

"Well, I'm looking for a couple of crowns."

"Crowns?"

"Yeah, you know, caps. People have them in their mouth covering teeth or implants."

"Oh, that's what they're called. I get it. Why do you want them, though?"

"It's complicated. I need them to figure out who those dead guys were, and why they were killed." Gabe nodded as if he understood, but his blank expression made me wonder if he did.

The best drink to have with a peanut butter and jelly sandwich was always a glass of cold milk. Unfortunately, I stopped buying milk when the cat walked out on me, but I did have coffee and I brewed a pot. Gabe drank it like I did—black, with two sugars.

I refilled our cups and reached into my pocket for my front door key. I slid it across the table. "Gabe, I'm going to be away for a few days. I'd like you to stay here and watch over the place while I'm gone."

He shook his head. "I can't do that, Rick."

"What? Why not?"

"I used to have a place just like this over on Sacramento Street. I loved that apartment, but I lost it when I lost everything else. I had a breakdown, Rick—a bad one. If I get a taste of my old life right now, it'll kill me."

I wasn't sure if this was the right time, but I was about to make a big commitment to Gabe, and I had to know about his past. "Gabe, at dinner the other night you began telling me about your previous life, but you didn't finish. Any chance you could right now?"

He was quiet, and I imagined the gears of his gray matter meshing together. "I met a guy," he said. "He loved fast food and came to the store a couple times a week. I guess he liked the way I paid special attention to the customers and he offered me an opportunity of a lifetime. He was a stockbroker at Merrill Lynch, and they had an intern program without any prerequisites. He got me into it and six months later I was a stockbroker—one of the few who got into the business without a college degree. I was one of Merrill's up and coming stars until I committed the cardinal sin. I sold short a couple hundred-thousand shares of a company's stock for a guy and three weeks later, when the company went bankrupt, he made over eight million dollars."

"I don't get it. Isn't that what a broker is supposed to do?"

"Yeah, it is, but I was so excited about getting the commission, I didn't exercise due diligence. That guy had insider information, and the SEC found out about it, and sent him to jail for a year. I got off easy. Merrill fired me, and the SEC barred me from ever selling securities again."

He took a deep breath and his pain cut through me like a sharp knife. "I didn't have a college education," he said. "No skills other than brokerage sales. Within three months, with my savings gone, I hit the bottle. Three months after that, I was homeless."

"Oh, man, I'm so ...so sorry."

"No need. I used up the feeling sorry stuff ...all by myself. Look, Rick, I'm sick. Sick in the head. I can't pick myself up, I've tried ...several times. I failed every time."

I didn't know what to say, but I knew what I thought—there but for the grace of God go I. If it weren't for my parents having some money and sending me to college, I could be in his shoes right now. "Do me a big favor, Gabe," I said. "I need someone to watch my place. So, do it as a favor to me, and when I get back, I'll help you give your life another try."

He walked to the window and stared out at the view of the bay. I couldn't see his face, but I knew he was crying. "Rick, don't get involved with me. There's more I haven't told you."

I didn't care. I knew at that moment I wanted to save this guy—more than I had even wanted to save my marriage. "I don't give a damn what you haven't told me. Just tell me you'll stay here for a few days."

Twenty-seven

I gave Gabe some cash for groceries and instructions not to open the door for anyone, then I hopped in a cab for the airport. Alex had already checked in and was sipping coffee from a Starbucks cup when I arrived at the El Al ticket counter. It was the first time I'd seen her not dressed in a business suit and heels; she was wearing Nike joggers, a sweatshirt with an 'I love San Francisco' logo and a pair of slip-ins. "I thought maybe you stood me up," she said.

I peeked at my watch. I was almost forty-five minutes late. "Sorry, I have a houseguest...had a hard time getting out."

Our flight was called for boarding at seven-thirty and to my surprise we were seated in business class. I looked at Alex. "I think Stella went over budget when I asked her to book this flight. Sorry."

Alex laughed. "It wasn't Stella, it was me. I told her to do it. Fourteen hours is too long in economy." Seven hours into the flight, it began to turn dark outside, and we reclined our seats to catch some sleep. I'd fantasized about sleeping next to Alex, but it was never on a Boeing 747.

The cab ride from Ben Gurion airport to the Sheraton Tel Aviv took about thirty-five minutes, most of which were monopolized by the driver, who apparently practiced his English on every American fare. When he pulled up to the hotel, he froze the meter at 142.2.

"I hope that's not dollars," I said.

He let out a belly laugh. "That for me it is shekels. For my American friends, I make it forty-dollars." I gave him fifty and told him to keep it. He smiled and said, "Have a day that is nice."

The hotel registration became a major catastrophe—somehow Stella had reserved only one room with a single queen and, fantasies aside, I wasn't about to jeopardize my relationship with Alex by sharing a one-bed hotel room with her. "We'll need two rooms," I said to the desk clerk.

The clerk winced. "I am sorry, sir. We have a tour this week that has taken all our rooms." Thinking it was the usual tourist shakedown, I pushed two twenties in his direction. He pushed them back. "I'm really sorry, sir."

I stuffed the bills back in my pocket. "Is there anything you can do for us?"

He scrolled his computer screen up and down, down and up. "Don't tell my manager," he said. "But at three o'clock, I will give you a two-bedroom suite for the price of two rooms."

I looked at Alex. She nodded. "We'll take it," I said. It later turned out to be the bridal suite; the first time for Alex; the second time for me.

~ * ~

It seems a week earlier someone had tried to set off a bomb in front of the Mossad headquarters, so our cab had to let us off a block away next to a metal barricade manned by four soldiers—all holding Uzis.

The soldier giving most of the orders was a woman who had an insignia on her sleeve with a three-lined chevron featuring a maple leaf in the center—probably a high-ranking sergeant. As we approached, the men raised their weapons and the woman raised her hand. She spoke in Hebrew.

"English?" I asked.

"Credentials, please," she said.

We handed her our passports and our badges that identified us as San Francisco medical examiners. She examined the passports and looked up from them several times to match the photos with the faces. "Very flattering picture," she said to Alex as she handed it back. She didn't say anything to me, so I assumed my photo, which resembled a mug shot in a police lineup, didn't impress her.

One of the other soldiers scanned us with a handheld metal detector, then pointed down the block. "Keep your IDs out and proceed through the double doors," he said.

Once we were inside the building, another soldier matched our credentials to a list on a computer screen. When he was satisfied we belonged there, he pointed to an elevator beyond a walk-through metal detector. "Agent Katz is on the fourth floor."

The guard must have called ahead, because when we stepped off the elevator, a middle-aged guy with light blue eyes and salt and pepper hair greeted us with a thrust-out hand. "Dovid Katz," he said. "Thank you, Dr. Keller ...Dr. Rose ...for coming all this way."

Katz led us to a conference room, where we were seated at a table with him and two of his associates who were introduced as Agent Feldman and Agent Levy. A secretary knocked and brought in a pot of tea along with a plate of pastries.

Growing up in a Jewish household, I was used to the usual ethnic desserts like hamantaschen and rugelach, but the one I picked off this plate was different. It was cinnamon dough, rolled and baked with a generous amount of chocolate in its center. "These are really delicious," I said. "What are they?"

Katz picked one up and took a bite. "They're chocolate babkas. My mom always baked these for us on Friday morning to eat after the Sabbath." Alex, who I knew rarely ate sweets, reached for a second one.

Katz took a sip of tea, set down his cup, and folded his hands. He knew Alex was my boss and must have assumed it was she he should negotiate with. "So, Dr. Keller, tell me why you are here."

Alex gave Katz a dismissive gesture. "Dr. Rose is in charge of this case. I prefer you discuss it with him."

"Of course, forgive me," Katz said. Suddenly, I became more than just a baked goods connoisseur. "Dr. Rose, I'm curious. There are many people in Israel with the surname of Rose. Most have been shortened from their Eastern European originals. Has yours, by chance?"

"Rosenkofsky ...but don't tell my mom."

Katz smiled. "I have good friends who are Rosenkofskys."

I knew Katz was trying to create an ethnic bond between us and that didn't bother me, but I wasn't here to do an ancestry search and, other than the fact that we were both Jewish, I doubted we had anything else in common. "I'll mention that to my dad. Can we get back to the purpose for our visit?"

I guess I insulted Katz, because it seemed like the temperature in the room dropped ten degrees when he spoke. "Very well," he said. "I believe you have some questions about a case you think we may be involved in."

"I'm not sure involved is the right word," I said. "Responsible for, might be more accurate."

"Really ...and why is that?"
"Let's start with the two dead guys we have in our morgue."
"What about them?"
"We think they worked for you."
"Why would you think that?"
"They both had dental implants that came out of Department 18."
"Department 18? What is Department 18?"

I liked Katz. He had given me the impression that he was a straight shooter, but all of a sudden, he was playing dumb. Even a rookie like me could see that. "Never mind, do you want your guys back, or do we bury them in unmarked graves?"

Katz stood and Feldman and Levy followed suit. "Please excuse us for a few minutes," he said. The three men left the room.

Alex smiled at me as if I really was the guy on the white horse. "You struck a nerve," she said.

"I don't get it. According to that Israeli woman I talked to a week ago, it's a public secret that Department 18 is an arm of Mossad. Why deny it?"

"These guys are pros, Rick. We'll just have to hang around until they want to tell us what they want to tell us."

Alex and I sat for about ten minutes, eating babkas and sipping tea, before the Mossad trio came back to the table and settled into their respective seats. Katz resumed the conversation. "So, tell us again, why do you think they were Department 18 guys?"

I decided to answer that question with a question. "What brand of undershorts are you wearing?"

Katz looked at me as if I had just beamed down from the starship Enterprise. "Excuse me?" he said.

"Let me guess ...Orlebar Brown ...made in London and sold in Tel Aviv by Bond Menswear at Sheinkin Street 45."

That single sentence transformed me from a lunatic space traveler into a modern-day Houdini. Katz furrowed his brow. "How ...?"

"I'm guessing Department 18 gets a discount there. Look, Dovid ...can I call you Dovid?" I asked. He nodded. "Dovid, stop with the bullshit ...please. We know about Department 18, you know about Department 18 and we all know these guys worked for Department 18. Do you want them back or not?"

"Do you have the crowns?" he asked.

When I was young, my dad demonstrated to me the concept of leverage. He took a wrench and positioned it on different sides of a hex nut to show me which position provided the best mechanical advantage. I realized, in this meeting at this moment, I had the wrench in the best position. I had the leverage and it was my turn to play dumb. "What crowns?" I answered.

"The ones that were on those implants you've been talking about. Do you have them?"

I turned the wrench one notch. "Before we talk about the crowns, let's talk about your fellow agent who offered me a bribe for them and then threatened my life if I wouldn't take it."

Katz looked at Feldman; Feldman looked at Levy and Levy looked backed at Katz. They reminded me of Moe, Larry, and Curly working out a plan that would inevitably get them into trouble. Katz eventually looked in my direction. "Is that the guy you asked me about when you called from the States?"

"That's the guy ...Ari Levine."

The Mossad agents exchanged looks again, but this time less obtrusively. Levy spoke for the first time. "Dovid had me run a check. We don't have an agent by that name."

Questions raced through my mind. Who the hell is Ari Levine? Who does he work for? Why does he want the John Doe crowns? Why does Katz want the crowns? Why do the goons want the crowns? Is my life in danger? Is Alex's? And then, the most important question of all—are these guys really telling us the truth?

Katz took the conversation back from Levy, while Feldman stayed mute as he had through the entire meeting. "Let's assume, just for argument's sake, that those two dead men did work for us. Would you entertain a deal for those crowns?" Katz asked.

I wondered what the word, deal, meant when negotiating with spies, but as long as they thought I had the crowns, we were still in charge. Before I could answer, Alex stepped back in to the conversation. "What kind of deal?" she asked.

"Give us the crowns and we'll give you the dead men's birth certificates. We get what we want and you get what you want."

This trade sounded amazingly familiar. "Ari Levine offered the exact deal," I said. "Only he was willing to throw in two hundred and fifty thousand dollars."

Katz didn't appear happy with the direction the conversation was heading. "So, is this negotiation about money?" he asked.

"No, it's about honesty. Who's Ari Levine?"

"I told you. I don't know who he is."

I began to question myself again. Perhaps I was making too big an issue over Ari Levine. Did it really matter to us who he is? Our job was to identify two dead bodies and Katz was willing to help us do that. But there was one small detail. We didn't have the capital to make a deal; we didn't have the crowns.

I snuck a look at Alex and her expression displayed concern. I surmised it was the same concern I was feeling. "We'll think about," she said.

Alex stood and I followed. "Thanks for the babkas," I said.

Katz threw up his hands. "Hey, what's the rush? Can't we at least set up another meeting for tomorrow?"

I knew Alex was buying us time. "We'll call you in the morning," she said.

Twenty-eight

Alex and I hadn't slept more than five hours since leaving San Francisco and we were both beat. I peeked at my watch. It was one-thirty and, unfortunately, the suite we were promised wouldn't be ready until three. "How about we get a bite and then head back to the hotel," I said.

Alex nodded. "Sounds good. Except for those babushkas, we haven't eaten in twelve hours."

"Babkas," I said. "The pastries were babkas, not babushkas." Alex broke out laughing and so did I. We laughed until tears rolled down our cheeks.

I asked the cab driver to choose a spot for us to have lunch and he dropped us at Manta Ray, a middle-eastern seafood restaurant on Alma beach overlooking the Mediterranean. The moment we spoke to the maître d', he pegged us for Americans, and I assume Americans are known to eat well and tip big. He led us to a table near the sand, where he snatched off a reserved placard and seated us facing the breaking waves.

It was quite a romantic setting. One which in my younger days would have prompted me to order a couple bottles of expensive wine to impress my date and then refill our glasses for an hour or two to seal the deal. But those days were long gone and Alex was not my date, so we ordered two iced teas and asked for the menus. A waiter placed them in front of us, Alex took one look and said, "Can you read Hebrew?"

When I was twelve years old, my mom and dad told me it was time to begin studying for my bar mitzvah—a religious initiation ceremony for a Jewish boy who had reached the age of thirteen. The idea of receiving presents and money had appealed to me, but learning how to read Hebrew had not. I put up a fight, but I knew it was hopeless. I agreed to meet with the rabbi twice a week, which seemed like forever, in order to learn how to read Hebrew. On Sabbath morning, April 18, 1998, I recited several Hebrew passages from the torah.

I smiled at Alex. "Yeah, I can read it, but can I understand it? No, I can't." I caught the waiter's eye and asked for menus printed in English. Alex ordered a sea bass filet served with eggplant and coriander butter and I went for the chunks of grouper cooked with a confit of garlic and fish stock. We spent a wonderful hour and a half—eating, talking and laughing—until my cynical side crept in and made me wonder if this was the lull before the storm.

Our suite was ready at three o'clock. When we checked in, the concierge handed me a sealed envelope. "Dr. Rose, this was left for you."

Alex looked at me. "Do you know anyone in Tel Aviv?" I didn't, so I just shook my head. When we were settled into the suite, I poured us two sparkling waters from the mini-bar and we sat on the couch to see what was in the envelope. It was a single piece of note paper, handwritten in English: *Meet me. The bar at Sam's Place. 11:00 p.m. 'Feldman.'*

"Feldman?" Alex said. "What's with this cloak and dagger stuff all of a sudden? He didn't say one word at the meeting this morning."

"Apparently, he was saving it for tonight."

~ * ~

Alex caught a nap in her bedroom, and I fell asleep on the couch. Around eight o'clock, we both woke with a start when the house phone rang. I got to it on the sixth ring. A man's voice said, "Do you have a pen?"

I glanced down at the desk. "Yeah, what's the message?"

"Same time—new location. Bird Head Bridge pedestrian walkway ... south end." The phone clicked and the voice was gone.

"Who was that?" Alex asked.

"Someone with a new location for the meeting."

"Feldman?"

"I don't know ...maybe ...we've never heard him speak."

"Why would he change the spot at the eleventh hour?"

I didn't answer because I knew Alex and I were thinking the same bad thoughts. After five minutes of silence, she said, "Rick, we're in over our heads. Do you think we should call the American embassy?"

"And say what? We're a couple of docs from the U.S. who got involved in some spy shit and we'd like them to call the Mossad and tell them we're sorry?"

"Well, when you put it that way, it does sound a little lame. Do you have a better idea?"

It was at this point that I wished I'd become a plumber—eight to five, four weeks' vacation, health insurance and oh, yeah ...no dead bodies. "I'll go alone," I said. "You stay here and we'll check in by cellphone every thirty minutes. If we lose contact, then you call the embassy and wiggle your way inside by pleading stupidity."

"So, you think we're really in danger here?"

"I don't know. Maybe Feldman just wants a recommendation for a good restaurant in San Francisco, but I doubt it. Let's just play it the way I said."

"Rick, I hired you to identify corpses, not to become one. I can't let you go to that meeting."

"Well, I'm going."

"I'm still your boss, and I say you're not."

"Look, Alex, you charged the room on the department's credit card and I already have my plane ticket home, so if you fire me, it's no big deal. Just make sure I qualify for unemployment insurance ...please."

Then Alex did the damnedest thing. She leaned over and kissed me on the cheek. "Rick, I'm not going to fire you. You're the most courageous, chivalrous man I've ever met."

I wanted to tell her I wasn't really that guy. I was a wimp who was scared out of his mind, but I didn't want to ruin the moment, so I said, "Thanks, Alex, I'll try not to let you down."

Twenty-nine

The weather had turned cold; I pulled on a wool turtleneck and slipped into my hooded windbreaker. We synched the times on our phones, and Alex walked me to the door. "Every thirty minutes," she said.

"Or sooner," I said. We both stood there with blank faces—no smiles, no tears, just sober expressions. We were both scared. Alex was scared for me and, as selfish as it may sound, I was scared for me, too.

I didn't think a goodbye kiss was appropriate so I gave Alex a hug and she hugged me back. I opened the door to leave, but she wouldn't let go. We held each other for a full minute before I broke loose and left for what I hoped would be my first and last clandestine rendezvous.

By the time I stepped outside the hotel, it had begun to drizzle and the cold temperature had created a low-level fog. A mental picture of Rick Blaine, Humphrey Bogart's character in the movie *Casablanca*, flashed through my mind. "I'm Rick Rose, not Rick Blaine," I muttered to myself. Then I broke out laughing. I wasn't even Rick Rose; actually, I was Richard Rosenkofsky.

The doorman hailed a cab and a white four-door Mercedes pulled to the curb. The driver didn't bother to get out. He just dropped the passenger window down and asked in English, "Where to?"

"Bird Head Bridge," I said.

"Get in."

I slipped into the back seat at the same time as the driver pushed down the flag on the meter. "You speak English," I asked.

"Yeah, I spent two years in New York."

"Really? What were you there for?"

"Uh, it was sort of a training deal."

"Really. For what?"

"Uh, management. The company wanted me to be a manager."

"So, why are you still behind the wheel?"

"I, uh, didn't like it. Say, what part of the bridge are you going to?"

"The south end of the pedestrian walkway."

I glanced at my phone. It had been almost a half hour since I left the room, so I hit the speed dial for Alex and she answered on the first ring. "Is everything all right?"

"It's fine. I'm almost there. Talk to you in a half hour."

The drizzle turned to rain and the streetlights became less frequent as we got closer to the Yarkon river. By the time the driver pulled to a stop at the edge of the roadway, it was pitch black and raining cats and dogs. "Dollars or shekels?" he asked.

I knew the bridge was out there, but I couldn't see it. My worst fears began to creep into my psyche, and my fight-or-flight response was screaming at me to flee. I opened the door to get a better look and I was hit with a stench from the river that smelled like rotten eggs mixed with bathroom sanitizers. "Take me back to the hotel," I said.

The cabbie, who up till this point seemed like pleasant guy, instantly changed his demeanor. "Get out, man. You asked me to take you here and now you're here. I have other fares to attend to."

"Well, I'm one of your fares, and I want you to drive me back to the hotel."

The driver stepped out of the car, exposing his full stature. He was about six foot four and easily weighed two-sixty. He yanked my door open and pulled me out. "Enjoy your walk," he said. Then he drove off without being paid.

It took about two or three minutes for my eyes to accommodate to the darkness and when they did, I spotted a figure approaching from the walkway that paralleled the bridge. I took off running, not knowing where to, but anywhere away from that bridge would do.

The road was slick. I stepped on a piece of loose blacktop and I fell face first into a water-filled pothole. My left cheek felt like it had been scraped with a piece of number 40 sandpaper, but I picked myself up and kept running. I glanced behind me. I could hear footsteps, but I couldn't see anyone. I sloshed on through the puddles until a small cluster of lights appeared up ahead. I broke into a sprint and headed for them.

The lights turned out to be a gas station with an attached convenience store. I stepped inside. The clerk took one look at my mud splashed face and reached into a drawer and withdrew a pistol. He yelled something in Hebrew, which, obviously I didn't understand. "English?" I asked.

He shook his head and waved the gun in the direction of the door. I held up my hands in the surrender position and backed toward it. My phone rang, but I was afraid to reach for it, so I continued to shuffle backwards toward the door until I could step outside.

Whoever was following me was probably out in the darkness, but not that far out. I scrambled for my phone and in my haste, dropped it onto the concrete. I picked it up; it had landed face down and the glass screen looked like a cluster of cobwebs. With the screen destroyed, I couldn't get to my address book or my speed dial, but I was hoping I could still tap in a number. But what was Alex's number? I couldn't remember.

In spite of the freezing temperature, I was sweating like a pig. What's her number? I asked myself. What's her number? Then it hit me. I tapped in *69 and the phone automatically dialed my last call.

Alex answered. "Where are you? It's been almost forty minutes."

"I don't know. Use the GPS on your phone to locate me and get a cab down here as fast as you can." I saw movement in the darkness. "Alex ...as fast as you can."

I shoved the phone into my pocket and pulled out a U.S. one-hundred-dollar bill. I stepped back inside the store, with my hands in the air, waving the currency. The clerk raised his pistol and motioned me to kneel. I could tell he was weighing the value of the money against the possibility of me being a threat. Apparently, the money won out and he approached me, snatched the bill and stood back. I laid face down and waited.

Within fifteen minutes, the door opened and the sound of a man's shoes echoed along the floor. I was afraid to look up, but I knew I had to. It was the hotel's concierge. He spoke Hebrew to the clerk and then English to me, "Let's get out of here," he said.

The taxi's engine was running and as soon as we slid into the back seat, it took off. Alex was there and gave me my second hug of the night. "Oh, God, I thought …"

I put my finger to her lips. "I'm fine. We'll talk when we get back to the hotel."

Thirty

It was after midnight when we stepped back into our suite and by the way Alex snuck a look at the mini-bar, I could tell she needed a drink. "Go ahead," I said.

"I know you're recovering. Would it bother you?"

"How did you know?"

"It's pretty obvious, Rick, I just don't want to tempt you."

She had no idea how much she was tempting me, and it had nothing to do with alcohol. I stepped to the fridge and took out a miniature Bombay Sapphire and a non-alcoholic beer. "I'll make you a martini. This O'Doul's works for me."

We sat on the couch sipping our drinks for a few minutes before Alex asked the inevitable question. "What happened out there? You look awful."

"It was a setup. Even the cab driver was a phony."

"You think Feldman was behind it?"

I hadn't had time to really analyze the night's disaster, so I closed my eyes and rested my head against the back of the couch. When my thoughts fell into place, I looked up. "It's possible, but not likely. We hardly know Feldman ...no ...we don't know him at all. If someone wanted to lure me into a meeting, it would have been Katz or at least his number two guy—Levy."

Alex took a sip from my homemade martini and held up the glass. "Delicious," she said.

I had to laugh. I didn't have any vermouth, and I didn't have any olives, so the martini I made was basically gin on the rocks. "Secret formula," I said. "You know, Alex, we don't know if that note was actually written by Feldman. All we know is his name was on it."

"But, why would Katz or Levy want to harm you? They want those crowns. They need you in order to get them."

"I don't know—maybe they think scare tactics will work," I said.

While we sat in silence and pondered the possibilities, we were startled by the shrill ring of the house phone. I looked at Alex and Alex looked at her watch. "It's almost one-thirty," she said.

"What d'ya think? Should I answer it?" I asked.

"If you don't, you'll be up all night wishing you had."

I grabbed the phone. "Who is this?"

"It's me," the caller said.

"Who's me?"

"Feldman. You didn't show up. Why?"

"I was at the bridge at eleven, just like you said."

"I didn't say anything about a bridge, I said the bar at Sam's Place."

The neurons floating around my brain started to piece together. "What time do the bars close in Tel Aviv?" I asked.

"Usually when the sun comes up," Feldman answered.
"Are you still there?"
"Yes. Why?"
"I'll be there in thirty minutes."

~ * ~

Unless you get into an argument with a drunk, a bar is a pretty safe place for a meeting, so when Alex insisted on going with me, I didn't put up a fight. I took a navy shower and threw on some clean clothes. "Let's go," I said.

We grabbed a taxi in front of the hotel and fifteen minutes later, to my surprise, we pulled up next to the American embassy. I leaned over the front seat to talk to the driver. "I said Sam's Place, not the embassy."

He laughed. "It is two doors down. Sam's is an American bar next door to the American embassy."

When we entered Sam's Place it did have a familiar feel to it. The walls were covered with murals of New York City, New Orleans, and San Francisco and the menu over the bar listed hamburgers, hot dogs and buffalo wings as the specials of the day.

We spotted Feldman sitting in a corner, worked our way through the late-night crowd and sat next to him. "Better late than never," I said.

"Glad you made it," he answered. "Something to drink?"

Alex stepped up. "Two sparkling waters with limes."

After the drinks arrived, Feldman said, "What was the confusion? What's with a bridge?"

"Someone called and said the meeting spot had been changed to the Bird Head Bridge. Who else knew you were meeting with me?"

The blood drained from Feldman's face and dots of perspiration formed on his upper lip. "Uh, no ...no one. Dammit, my phone was tapped." He stood and performed a three-sixty scan of the room and then sat back down. "Let's do this quickly," he said. "When Katz and Levy told you the Mossad did not have an agent named Ari Levine, they weren't telling you the whole truth."

Alex wrinkled her brow. "What do mean? Do they, or don't they?"

Feldman downed two fingers of Scotch and closed his eyes as the liquor worked its way down his throat. "Ari and I were good friends," he said. "We went through the academy together and worked out of the same office for fifteen years. Ari spoke perfect Farsi and two years ago, he was picked for an undercover assignment in Iran. A double agent betrayed him, and he was arrested in Tehran. The Iranian government hung him on December 16th, 2017."

Alex leaned over and squeezed Feldman's hand. "That's terrible. I'm so sorry."

"Why are you telling us this?" I asked

Feldman's voice cracked when he answered. "The Mossad would never admit that Ari had been an Israeli spy. They wouldn't even admit he ever existed. My good friend was erased from all the Israeli records as if he had never been born. When you brought up his name, I decided I couldn't be party to that charade any longer. I'm telling you this out of love for my friend, Ari Levine."

"So, who do you think is using his name?"

"Who do I think? I don't think ...I know. This man is an Iranian spy who is using the name Ari Levine, because he knows Mossad will never admit he's impersonating one of their own."

"But he knows everything Mossad knows. How ...?"

"I'm not surprised. We listen in on Iran, and they listen in on us. We feed each other false information along with the truth ...it's a guessing game."

I never would have made it to graduation day in spy school. This was crazier than my ex-wife's concept of fertilization. "Why do Dovid Katz and Ari Levine's impersonator want those crowns?"

Feldman's eyes turned to slits. "Dr. Rose, you know I can't tell you that. I'm not a traitor to my country, I'm just a man who wants his friend remembered."

I respected Feldman. I wanted to think if I were in his shoes, I would have acted with as much courage and as much love as he did. I knew I wouldn't have, though, because down deep I wasn't a very brave guy. "Are you in danger?" I asked.

He looked around the room for a second time. "Maybe, but maybe not. Because Ari Levine never existed. Did he?"

Thirty-one

I had promised Alex the trip to Tel Aviv and back would only take three days. Our plane was scheduled to depart for San Francisco at ten-thirty the next morning, but Alex was concerned that we hadn't settled anything with Dovid Katz. "Maybe we should stay over another day," she said.

"What for?"

"To close the deal for the return of the bodies."

"Alex, we don't have those crowns. That's what the deal was all about for Katz."

"So, we just leave without contacting him?" she said.

"Exactly. Look, he's not going to let this go. My guess is our next meeting with him will be in San Francisco. In the meantime, maybe we can find those damn crowns."

I'm not sure Alex was convinced that my decision to 'get outta Dodge' was the correct one, but she had faith in me, and agreed to start packing. If only I had as much faith in myself.

Ben Gurion airport was packed with people jabbering in a dozen different languages. Hebrew was the dominant one, but I recognized some Arabic, Farsi, Turkish and, of course, English. The ticket agent spoke all of them and used her English to get us pointed in the right direction.

We reached our gate about a half hour before departure and were greeted by Dovid Katz and his sidekick Agent Levy. "What's the hurry to leave?" Katz asked.

"The babkas gave me an intestinal problem," I said.

Katz laughed. "I doubt that very much. What's the real reason?"

Anger boiled up inside me. "I didn't like being lied to and then being intimidated at the Bird Head bridge."

"I don't know what you're talking about."

I pushed my face into Katz's as far as I could without kissing him. "You're a fucking senior agent in one of the leading intelligence agencies on this planet. You know what I'm talking about and if you don't ...you should."

The last call was made for our flight, and Alex tugged on my sleeve. "We have to go," she said.

I handed Katz my business card. "When you're through jerking us around, give me a call." I turned and followed Dr. Keller down the jetway to the waiting plane.

~ * ~

Close to twenty-four hours later, I dragged myself up the stairs to my apartment. The hour was late so rather than use my spare key and scare Gabe, I knocked lightly on the door to alert him. There was no response. I knocked again; this time with my fist—still no reply. I used my key and stepped inside.

I expected the worst, but the apartment was clean and tidy. I remembered that during my first day on the job, Alex had introduced me as the new 'mouth mechanic.' It had such a clever ring to it that I had a notepad made with the silhouette of a wrench wrapped around a tooth. Gabe had written his goodbye on one of the sheets. It read: *Rick, I appreciate your help, but I don't deserve it. Please don't look for me. I'm nothing but trouble for you. P.S. a guy beat on the door for twenty minutes, but I didn't open it. He yelled his name was Jake.* My spare housekey was set next to the note.

I don't know if it's because of flying east to west or because the customs guys choose to hassle you at two in the morning, but it always seems that jet lag is worse coming back to the U.S. This trip was no exception.

I managed to will myself out of bed by eleven, but it felt like I hadn't slept at all. I showered and shaved, drank two cups of coffee, and then Ubered to work. Old reliable Stella was busy at her desk when I walked in. "Welcome back," she said. "I heard I screwed up the hotel reservations."

"No problem. I guess Alex is already here, huh?"

"She was here when I got in at eight."

It's often said that women are the stronger sex, and Alex proved it to me this morning. As usual, I asked Stella if there were any messages.

"The same old usual suspects—Joselle Freeman Rosenkofsky and Ari Levine... five times," she said.

Suddenly, I had a bad headache. "You have any Tylenol?" I asked. Stella opened her top drawer and handed me a bottle. I shook out three tablets, swallowed them without any water and handed it back. "So, how's the romance?"

"You mean Chris from the dating app?"

"Is there another?"

"No, just him. He's great. We're seeing each other again tonight."

"Well, have fun, but hold out for a good dinner first."

"Oh, Rick, you're so old fashioned."

I sat at my desk and pondered how I had gone from a hip dentist at twenty-eight to an old fashioned odontologist at thirty-four. I didn't have time to solve the conundrum; my intercom buzzed. I pushed the blinking button. "Yeah, Stella, what's up?"

"Joselle Rosenkofsky is on line one."

I reluctantly answered the call. "Goddammit, Josie, stop using my father's name."

"I like it. It reminds me of the day we met."

I wasn't in the mood to go down memory lane with my ex-wife. "I'm busy. What d'ya want?"

"It's Tuesday."

"So?"

"So, you missed our appointment last Friday with Dr. Rosenberg."

"Oh, that. I was out of the country."

"Well, I made a new one for tomorrow."

"That's nice, let me know how it goes."

"Rick, you promised."

"So did you when you said 'forever in sickness and in health.'"

"But you said you'd come with me."

I was getting tired of listening to Josie whine. "Well, I lied. I'm very busy right now. Goodbye."

Thirty-two

Between four years of dental school and six years of private practice, I had probably placed a couple thousand crowns on back teeth without raising any concerns. Now, two crowns I didn't even place were driving me nuts. They were so special that someone committed murder to get hold of them, but who had them now? Not Israel or Iran—they both wanted to get their hands on them. Another player, someone the goons work for, wants them also. Common sense was telling me maybe it was time to find out who that someone was.

I dialed Jim's cell number. He must have been expecting a call from someone important, because when he answered, his voice was strictly business. "Detective James Allen speaking."

"Jim, it's me, Rick Rose."

He sounded disappointed that he had wasted all that energy. "Oh, it's you. What's doin'?"

"I need some police work done."

"Yeah? So why call me?"

"Well, last time I checked your title, you were a policeman."

"I mean, why me?"

"Well, theoretically, you're assigned to our case, and if I'm not mistaken, Alex asked you to give me all the help you can."

"That was before."

"Before what?"

"Before you accused me of leaking your shit to the bad guys."

"I thought you got over that."

"I reconsidered. I want another apology."

I admit I did accuse Jim and then tried to trivialize it, but I thought by now he was over it. Apparently, he was still pushed out of shape. "I apologize," I said. "I was out of line. Totally out of line."

The phone was silent and I knew Jim was deciding whether to help me or throw me to the wolves. "Okay, what d'ya want?" he asked.

"There's a new Mercedes model that came out this year—the Maybach GLS 600 4MATIC. Can you find out how many are registered in and around San Francisco?"

"Yeah, I guess I could do that."

"Great, that's great. And while you're at it, could you give me a list of the owners and their addresses?"

"Maybe I should interview them for you, too."

"Would you?"

"Fuck, no. I'll have the list for you tomorrow."

~ * ~

I gave Stella my notes from the Israel trip to type into a report, and then I caught the elevator to the basement. When I opened the door to the morgue, I knew Helmut was in surgery; a Bach concerto was turned up to max volume.

I tapped on the pathologist's shoulder and his head snapped up so hard, I thought he would break his neck. "Rick, please don't interrupt me that way," he yelled above Johann Sebastian's *Fugue in D minor*.

I wasn't sure what mode of interruption he preferred, so I just apologized and pointed toward his desk. He turned off the speakers and joined me there. "What can I do for you?" he asked.

"Alex and I went to Tel Aviv for a few days to get some info on the John Does."

"Oh, wow. What did they say?"

"Not much. They want those crowns that are missing from our cadavers."

"But you don't have them?"

"Well, they think I do."

"Why would they think that?"

"Because I led them to."

Helmut nodded as if he understood, but his eyes had a glazed-over look to them. I admit I knew very little about espionage, but in the land of the blind, the one-eyed man is king, so in this morgue I guess I was perched upon the throne. "Has anyone approached you about this case?" I asked.

"Approached? I don't understand."

"I have people pressuring me for those crowns. I was wondering if you have the same."

Helmut smiled. "I'm invisible, Rick. I can go to dinner with two other people, and not one even notices I'm there until the check arrives. I'm the last guy anyone would think to get information from."

I really felt sorry for him. Probably his only acquaintances were the subjects he dissected. "Let's you and I get a meal together sometime," I said.

His smile turned ear to ear. "I'd like that, Rick. Yes, I'd like that very much. Anytime."

~ * ~

Alex's secretary told me to go right in, but sharing a suite for a couple nights didn't give me entitlement, so as usual I knocked. "It's open," she said.

I peeked around the door. "Hi, roomie."

Alex laughed and motioned me to take a seat. "How are you feeling?" she asked.

"Like I haven't slept in three nights."

"Have you?"

"I got a couple hours last night. My brain won't turn this case off."

"I get it. I never told you, Rick, but I wasn't sure you would have the balls to stand up to a guy like Katz. You're my role model."

Role model? I'd never been called that. Even though I knew it was a misnomer, it had a nice ring to it, especially coming from a classy lady like Alex. "Yeah, I'll have to set up a time for autographs."

"You're too hard on yourself. Someday you'll realize that."

Now I was getting a little embarrassed, so I changed the subject to the real reason for my visit. "I've been thinking. Somewhere between Ari Levine, Dovid Katz and Jake what's his name, lies the answer to why we're digging around in this dung pile."

"How do we dig ourselves out?"

"Jim is checking out the car that dumped the bodies, and I'm going to work on Ari and Jake."

Alex frowned. "That's dangerous, Rick."

"Not as long as they think I have the crowns."

And then, I got my second kiss from Alex. It was planted squarely on my left cheek. "Be careful," she said.

Thirty-three

Probably in the espionage world this was a normal happening, but I found it interesting that Ari Levine, who most likely was an Iranian spy, had a phone number with an Israel country code and two others with Los Angeles and D.C. area codes, and yet whenever I called, he answered from somewhere in San Francisco.

I decided to use his L.A. number, which went immediately to voicemail: *You've reached Ari. Leave a message.*

"Hey, Ari, I heard you're trying to get ahold ..."

The phone clicked. "Rick, is that you?"

"Yeah, my secretary said you called."

"Several times. Hey, I think I scared you off last time we met. I apologize."

It's easy to show bravado when you're not engaging face to face. "Scared? You didn't scare me ...just surprised me."

"Okay, I'm glad to hear that. Can we get together again?"

"Sure. Where?"
"Do you like Van Gogh?"
"Never met him."
Ari laughed. "Are you ever serious?"
"I am now. What about Van Gogh?"
"The De Young is exhibiting his stuff. Meet me in front of The Potato Eaters at two o'clock."

I looked at my watch; it was getting close to one—lunchtime. About a block away from the office there was a little hole-in-the-wall where a man named Babak ran a soup restaurant. It wasn't really a restaurant—more like a take-out with an eight-seat counter for people who wanted to hang around. He was an Iranian guy who identified as Persian, and who charged an arm and a leg for a medium sized bowl of flavors that most Americans had never tasted. Between eleven and two, there was a constant line of customers who waited up to a half an hour for the privilege of spending sixteen dollars for the soup of the day.

I took my place at the end of the line and strained my neck to peek around the crowd for a glimpse of the menu blackboard. Today's one and only was *Ash Reshteh,* a Persian noodle soup made with lentils, veggies and a variety of herbs topped with caramelized onions. Along with a Diet Coke and tax, my bill came to almost twenty-one dollars.

Most of the customers took their soup in Styrofoam containers to the nearby park or back to their office, but I spotted a guy leaving the counter, and I snatched the seat, and dug into Babak's thick creation. The bottom of the bowl appeared way too soon, and I used my single square of pita bread to mop up the remaining drops.

I was so focused on my lunch that I didn't notice two guys had somehow found seats at the counter—one on each side of me.

When I stood to leave, the one on my left grabbed my arm. "What's your hurry, Doc?"

It was Jake and his sidekick—the guy I had puked on. He opened his jacket just wide enough for me to see a pistol resting in a belt holster. "Hey, guys, I'd like to talk, but I have an appointment," I said.

Jake pushed me back on the stool. "You made us a promise and you never kept it. The appointment can wait. Where's the crown you promised us?"

There's a saying I once heard—never let them see you sweat—but unfortunately, my nervous system hadn't listened. A drop of perspiration hung off the tip of my nose until it finally dropped into the empty soup bowl. "It's in a safe place," I said.

"We want it, now or ..."

"Or what?" I asked. "Or you kill me?'

"Yeah, that's exactly what we'll do," Jake said.

I was getting just a little bit tired of this guy's empty threats and decided to let him know it. "We both know that's not going happen, so here's the deal, Jake. The crown is up for sale. I suggest you talk to your boss and find out how much you can afford to pay for it, because that's the only way you're going to get it. By the way, the bidding has started at two-hundred and fifty 'K.'"

Now the sweat began to drip off Jake's nose. "Is that what you were doing in Israel?" he asked.

"Who told you I was in Israel?"

"Never mind who told me. Is that why you were there?"

For the second time, I got up off my stool and this time no one pushed me back down. "Fuck you," I said. "You have twenty-four hours to make your bid, and it better be good or you lose. And if that happens, I'm guessing your boss isn't going to be very happy with you. Is he?" As I walked away, Jake and his buddy no longer looked intimidating.

~ * ~

The Van Gogh exhibit took up the entire second floor of the DeYoung Museum. The Potato Eaters was listed on the handout as #56. Ari Levine, dressed in his usual suit and tie, was seated on a bench directly in front of the painting. He had the look of an art critic, but no critic in his right mind would have the cajónes to criticize Van Gogh. "I don't like it," I said.

Ari didn't turn around. "Why is that?"

"Just a bunch of people eating dinner. Anyway, it's too dark. I like his impressionistic stuff."

"You know, he only sold one in his lifetime."

I really wasn't into art, but I recently read that an original Van Gogh had sold for over a hundred million dollars. "How much did he get for it?"

"Four hundred Francs—about twenty bucks."

I sat down next to Ari. "Speaking of sale prices, pitch me again."

"Two hundred and fifty thousand," he said.

"How?"

"What do you mean, how?"

"Do you give it to me in a suitcase or what?"

Ari chuckled. "We'll set up an account for you at my favorite vacation spot, the Casino de Monte-Carlo. As soon as you deliver the merchandise, I'll wire the money into your account right in front of your eyes. Withdraw it whenever you like."

"What about the IRS?"

"Declare it. You wouldn't be the first guy to get lucky at a craps table in Monaco."

I tried to figure out how one stalls when one has just been offered a quarter of a million dollars in cash. Then it occurred to me. "It sounds great, Ari, but ..."

"But, what?"

"Someone else has offered me more."

"How much more?"

Now it was my turn to chuckle. "Ya know Ari, that wouldn't be in my best interest to tell you. Would it?"

Ari bit his lip while his brain added up zeros. "Would five hundred do it?"

"Is that a question or an offer?"

"An offer."

I stood to leave. "Just like you, Ari, I have partners. I'll run this by them."

"I need to know soon."

For the second time in less than an hour, I realized I'd regained leverage. "Don't worry, I'll call you," I said. I left Ari alone with the Potato Eaters—a very dark painting.

Thirty-four

By four o'clock, jet lag had caught up with me, and I hit a wall. I needed sleep, and I needed it now. Off in the distance, I heard a voice. "Hey, Mac, wake up." I wanted to open my eyes, but they stayed glued shut and the voice returned. "Hey, asshole, I don't rent by the month." I ignored the voice and suddenly felt something dripping down my neck.

I woke with a start. The cab driver was emptying a water bottle over my head. "Where ...where am I?" I asked.

"You're home. You have been for twenty minutes. I restarted the meter so you owe me forty bucks ...cash."

I gave him two twenties and a ten-dollar tip, then struggled up the stairs to my apartment, where I collapsed on the couch. I had no idea how long I slept, but when my phone started to buzz, the apartment was pitch black and a ray of moonlight was peeking through the open curtains. I searched feverishly for my cell and found it wedged between two cushions. "Yeah, this is Rick," I answered.

A voice on the other end said, "I have the information you're looking for."

"Who ...who is this?"

"It's Jim."

"Jim? Jim who?"

"Jim Allen, you prick. What ...you fall off the wagon or somethin'?"

"No, no, sorry Jim, it's been a long day. What's up?"

"You want this DMV stuff or not?"

"Yeah, sure. Just email it to me, and I'll check it out in the morning."

"That won't work. I need to talk to you first."

I looked at my watch. It was twelve-twenty. "I'm pretty tired, Jim, can't it wait till tomorrow?"

"No, it's now or never."

"Okay. Okay, come on over."

I pulled myself off the couch and turned on the coffeemaker. While I was waiting for it to perk, I reread Gabe's note that was still resting on the table. *Rick, I appreciate your help, but I don't deserve it. Please don't look for me. I'm nothing but trouble for you* ...I shook my head. Something was off, but I didn't know what.

I managed to get a cup down before I opened the door for Jim. "You look like shit," he said.

"Yeah, nice to see you too. Want some coffee?"

"Got any cream?"

"No, I've been away. Everything's sour."

"Okay, black then."

I poured us each a cup and motioned Jim to one of my two chairs. "So, what's so important that you had to deliver this stuff in person?"

"I heard you and Alex got away together."

I was pretty sure where this was going to lead and I didn't like it. "Got away together? No, we went together to Israel ...on business."

"Monkey business, I'm thinkin'."

I really wasn't in the mood for a pissing contest with this guy. "Look, Jim, I would love to be in a relationship with Alex, but I'm not. It's strictly business. So, you can believe that or not; I really don't give a shit. All I want from you is help finding out who the John Does were and why they were killed. Do you think you can handle that?"

Jim's face, which was always a bit ruddy, turned crimson. "Yeah, I can handle it, but if I catch you getting cozy with Alex, I'll beat the shit outta you."

I should have let it go right there, but this macho prick was definitely pissing me off. I snatched the cup from his hand and tossed it into the sink where is exploded into little pieces. "I have news for you. You don't have veto rights over Alex's personal life and, for that matter, over mine either, so save the tough guy crap for your perps."

Jim, obviously, wasn't used to people pushing back. He grabbed the report he had placed on the table and headed for the door. "Fuck you," he said.

"You better leave me those papers," I yelled. "Or Dr. Keller will hear about it in the morning. Oh, and while I'm at it, maybe I'll fill her in on tonight's conversation. I'm sure she'd love to hear how you're protecting her."

Jim did a one-eighty and grabbed me by the collar. He had a crazed, out-of-control expression I'd only seen once before in my lifetime—when my uncle Frank was taken to the insane asylum. "You do, and I'll kill you," he said.

I pushed his hand away from my throat. "Okay, just give me the report." He dropped two papers on the table and slammed the door on his way out.

I figured I'd add Jim's warning to my list of death threats, but unlike the others, I took it more seriously. This one was rooted in passion rather than persuasion.

I spread out the sheets Jim had left behind. They were copies of computer printouts from the California Department of Motor Vehicles and listed every Mercedes-Maybach GLS 600 4MATIC that was registered in San Francisco and adjacent counties for the year 2019. I had googled the model a few weeks ago and knew it retailed for around 200k, so I figured there couldn't be more than one or two in the vicinity. I was wrong. Apparently, two-hundred thousand was no big deal for twenty-two buyers, six of whom were in the city of San Francisco. I set my coffee cup on top of the papers and went to bed. I slept for close to ten hours.

Thirty-five

I arrived at my office at noon, but nobody was around to notice. Stella was out to lunch, probably with her new boyfriend; Alex was attending a workshop, and Helmut most likely was holed up in the basement. Jim, the other member of the team, was *persona non grata* after having had another personal argument with Alex. I found it ironic that Jim, who had warned me to stay away from Alex, was himself ordered by her to do just that.

As I mentioned earlier, the DMV report listed six Mercedes-Maybach GLS 600 4MATIC owners who registered their vehicles in the city of San Francisco. To my surprise, Jim had gone above and beyond the call of duty by using his resources to match a phone number to each of the names.

The first two I checked out were registered to Prichard Motors, a high-end car dealer on Van Ness Avenue. When I inquired about the cars, I was told they were still in their inventory and available for a test drive, if I was interested. I told them to call me when they dropped the price about a hundred and fifty thousand.

The next one was registered to Raymond Eldridge, who turned out to be the city attorney and not a likely candidate for disposing of dead bodies.

Of the remaining three, two were owned by widows living in the prestigious Forest Hill neighborhood. When I called, I was told they both had chauffeurs who were allowed to drive the cars only when the women were in the back seats. That narrowed the list to one—a business named Fog City Car Service.

I grabbed a cab and had it drop me at Fourteenth and Mission, a half a block from Fog City. For a company that owned super expensive cars, the facility wasn't very impressive. There was an office that resembled a glorified kiosk and a fenced lot that housed only three cars: a Cadillac XT5 all-wheel drive, a BMW 430i coupe and a Lexus LS 500 sedan. There was no Mercedes in sight.

I stepped into the office. It was pretty stark. There were a metal desk, two card table chairs and a bunch of manila folders that were piled on the floor. A bald-headed guy with a cigar butt hanging from his lips looked up from his phone. "Help ya?" he asked.

"Yes, I was told you have a Mercedes-Maybach GLS 600 4MATIC for rent."

The guy spit some tobacco juice into an empty Pepsi can. "We don't rent cars; we partner with foreign tourists to provide transportation on a monthly basis."

"Sounds like you rent cars," I said.

The guy looked me up and down. I assume to assess if I had enough money to make it worth his while to talk with me. "The Maybach is out for a couple more weeks. How 'bout a Caddy?"

"I really wanted the Mercedes. So, it'll be back in two weeks?"

The guy rummaged through the stack of manila folders and pulled out the one on the bottom of the pile. "Eleven days, to be exact."

"Oh, that's too long to wait. How much is the Cadillac?"

"You a tourist?"

I nodded. "Yeah ...Denmark ...Copenhagen."

I guess that piqued his interest. "It's five grand a month. Ya want to see it?" he asked.

"Sure, can you bring it up front?"

I think my host smelled blood in the water or more likely, money in my pocket. He jumped out of his chair, snatched a set of keys from a corkboard and headed for the rear door. "Wait here, I'll bring it around," he said.

As soon the door slammed behind him, I grabbed the Mercedes folder from his desk and opened it. The top page was a bunch of disclaimers, but the next page was the rental agreement. The first line read: ...between lessor, Fog City Motors, 1273 Mission Street, San Francisco, CA and lessee, Robert Jones, 1520 Jackson Street, San Francisco, CA ...

I put on my readers to make sure I was seeing the lessee's address correctly because I lived at 1720 Jackson. I guess I stared too long, because when the front door opened, I was caught red-handed holding the folder. "What the fuck are you doing?" the car guy said.

I closed the folder and dropped it back on the desk. "Nothing. I just ...nothing ...really ...nothing."

"Are you here to rent a vehicle or are you just blowing smoke up my ass?"

I inched past him toward the open door. "Actually ...the latter." I gave a weak wave and sprinted down Mission Street.

Thirty-six

By the time I got back to my office, everyone, except Jim, of course, had returned. Stella looked up from some paperwork. "Where have you been? I haven't seen you all day," she said.

"Now, now, Stella, you're talking to the great... one and only forensic odontologist for San Francisco. He's a very important guy. Lots of stuff he has to do."

She rolled her eyes. "Yeah, okay ...sorry, I don't know what came over me. Dr. Keller asked that you check in with her as soon as you can."

"Thanks. So, another lunch with your new heart throb?"

"He's so cool, Rick. I want you to meet him."

Stella's intercom buzzed. "Is Dr. Rose back yet?" a voice asked.

I leaned into the speaker. "Just got back, Alex. I'll be right there." I did an about face, headed out the door, then peeked back in. "Let's you and I and Mr. Right have lunch soon."

Even though Alex and I had shared a hotel suite, and I knew that we were friends beyond being colleagues, I was still careful not to overstep my bounds. As usual, I knocked before stepping into her office.

"Rick, you're always welcome in here. You don't have to knock," Alex said.

"Hey, I'm an old school millennial. What can I say?" I took a seat facing her desk. "So, it sounds like something important has come up."

Alex's smile disappeared and was replaced by an expression of concern. "We've got a problem," she said.

"Should I down a double shot of Gatorade before you tell me?"

That brought back her smile. "Rick, you make me laugh. I love that."

"I'm glad, Alex. Let's hear about the problem."

"Well, you already know I don't want the feds or a bunch of local cops getting in our way here and that's why I put up with Jim Allen's narcissistic personality disorder. He stays out of the way and lets us do our work."

"You mean he's too lazy to do his job."

"It's a tradeoff, isn't it? We give him a case, we do the work, and as a reward for staying out of our hair, he gets the credit when we solve it."

"Oh, I didn't realize he gets a gold star when this is over."

Alex held up her hands like she was waiting for rain to fall. "Who cares? Do you?"

I hadn't really thought about it before, but I did now, and I came up with the same conclusion as Alex. "I couldn't care less. So, what's the problem?"

"I told Jim for the tenth time that we were done as a couple, but he wouldn't listen. I had him thrown out of the building."

"And he wants revenge?"

Alex nodded. "And his way of getting it is by bad mouthing me. His homicide captain announced that he's dropping by at four o'clock today to lecture me on the concept of obstruction of justice."

"Obstruction? What a joke. You want me here to back you up?"

"Would you?"

"Of course," I said. We spent the next hour working on strategy.

The captain wasn't due to arrive for another forty-five minutes, which gave me time to head down to the morgue, fill Helmut in on what was happening and prep him on what he should say if he was questioned. All of a sudden, I felt like a high-priced defense attorney from Manhattan rather than just an underpaid dentist from Brooklyn.

I rejoined Alex about ten minutes before the captain was due. At precisely four o'clock sharp, her secretary announced that he had arrived. My stereotypical thinking bit me in the ass again. I was expecting a short, overweight, gray-haired guy with a pot belly to step through the door, but in walked a six foot-two, good looking man who, judging by his physique, worked out at least five days a week.

He removed his hat, slipped it under his left arm and with the other, thrust out his hand to Alex. "Captain Kelly," he said. "It's a pleasure to finally meet you, Dr. Keller."

I could tell Alex was taken aback. We had prepped ourselves for war and assumed the captain would be our enemy, but when she shook his hand and let it linger for a few extra seconds, I knew that wasn't to be the case. "Please, call me Alex," she said.

He presented a wide smile and said, "I'm Mike."

How quickly one can go from the starting team to sitting on the end of the bench. I cleared my throat as loudly as I thought appropriate. Alex turned to me. "Oh, Mike, this is Dr. Rose, our forensic odontologist. I'm sure he won't mind if you call him Rick."

I shook his hand, but I didn't let it linger. "Of course," I said. "Rick is fine."

Alex's secretary brought in a carafe of coffee and a few pastries. Mike declined both, saying he was training for a marathon. I already hated this guy.

Alex sipped her coffee and went right to the point. "So, Mike, I was wondering if you were coming here today to slap my hands or arrest me for obstruction."

He laughed. "Neither, Alex. The obstruction comment over the phone was for Jim's benefit. He was sitting right next to me at the time of the call. I can understand why you want him off the case; he can be very overbearing."

"I don't really want him off the case," Alex said. "I just had to let him know that this is my turf and he has to respect it ...and that means me, too."

Mike looked at me. "Rick, what do you think of Detective Allen?"

"I think he's a prick, but he knows this case, and I think he should stay on it."

Captain Mike Kelly must have risen to his rank because he could read people. He read me like a book. "I know Jim's a lazy, corrupt cop and I know you know that too. Why do you really want him to stay on this case?"

I looked at Alex. Our plan was to build Jim up and beg to have him back on the case, but now, thanks to the captain, our strategy was out the window. Alex made the call. "Mike, you strike me as a straight shooter. Can I be totally honest with you?"

"Absolutely," he said.

Alex turned to me, I assumed for my approval. I nodded and she turned back to Kelly. "Rick has done more investigative work in a couple weeks than Jim Allen could do in a couple years. I want Jim back here because I don't want some other hotshot from homicide to bull his way in here and upset the apple cart."

The captain smiled. "So, you want a detective who doesn't detect."

"Right," she said. "As soon as Rick figures out who killed these guys and why, we'll turn everything over to Jim. He'll be in your office within ten minutes bragging about his detective work."

Mike nodded, sending the signal that he was on board, but something was bothering him. "I know a little about this case," he said. "Don't you think the CIA could best handle it?"

"You ever work with those spooks?" Alex asked.

Kelly broke out in a belly laugh. "Yeah, Alex, I have. Okay, we'll keep this in my department for now." He stood and lifted his hat from the table. "It was a pleasure meeting both of you. Detective Allen will be back on the case, with an apology, tomorrow morning."

Thirty-seven

As I left the building to go home, I thought about my visit to Fog City Motors. The guy who rented the Mercedes GLS 600 lives at 1520 Jackson Street. It wasn't too hard to connect the dots. What didn't jive was the renter's name. The guy who roughed me up definitely wasn't named Robert Jones and I doubt anyone else living there was named that either. It was obvious the Saudis didn't show much creativity when forging a name.

I hit my Uber app and I punched in my address—1720 Jackson—as my destination. A white Toyota rolled up four minutes later. "Rich?" The driver asked.

"Rick, not Rich," I said as I slid into the rear seat. "Hey, make sure you go straight up Jackson."

"It's faster to go up California and cut over."

"I know, but I want to go up Jackson."

"Time is money, Rich. I can't do that."

I passed a ten-dollar bill over the front seat. "This should cover gas for one extra block."

As we approached the fifteen hundred block, my driver screeched to a halt. As usual, limos and town cars were double parked for the next fifty yards.

"This is good," I said. "I'll walk the rest of the way." I hopped out, and the Toyota sped away.

The scene looked much the same as it had a few weeks earlier. The Mercedes were in the front of the line, the Cadillacs in the back and most of the chauffeurs were congregated in small groups.

I worked my way to the front of the line where, I knew from my last visit, the Saudi drivers were parked. Five chauffeurs were huddled together, each sucking on their cigarette. They ignored me as I approached. I knew they weren't a very friendly lot, but I had an idea that might help me penetrate their hostility.

I walked up to the group and handed each man one of my business cards. "Dr. Rose," I said. "Who called for an odontologist?"

The guys looked at the cards and went back to their smokes. "Talk to Moe," one said.

"Moe ...yeah, that's the guy who called. Where can I find him?" I asked.

The guy took one last drag and flicked his cigarette into the gutter. "You don't find Moe, he finds you," he said.

I had a feeling the guy who chased me away last time I was here was Moe. I really didn't want to face him again, but it was too late. The raging bull, who was barreling down from the mansion with two guys running shotgun behind him, was most likely Moe.

I figured a smile and a handshake was my best approach. I figured wrong. Moe cold-cocked me with one punch. When the stars disappeared, I sat up and blinked a couple times. Moe was standing over me and his two compadres were backing him up. One of them was Jake.

"What are you doing back here, asshole?" Moe asked.

I pointed to Jake. "I came to do business with that guy, but I guess he's not interested anymore."

Moe took Jake aside and they became embroiled in a heated discussion. When the cozy chat was over, Moe stepped back, gently took my arm and helped me to my feet. "So sorry, Dr. Rose. Karim vouched for you. Would you like to come inside the mansion for a cup of tea?"

The last place I wanted to be right now was inside a Saudi residence. I'd read what happened to people they didn't like. They ended up cut into small pieces that fit into a briefcase. "No, thank you," I said. I nodded toward Jake. "Karim and I can talk tomorrow."

I began to wobble away, but Karim quickly caught up with me. "I hope this doesn't affect our deal for that crown. I have a very good offer for you."

"Oh, yeah? How much?" I asked.

"Seven-fifty."

"Thousand?"

"Yes, Dr. Rose, cash ...seven-hundred and fifty thousand."

I handed him my business card. "Call me tomorrow," I said.

Thirty-eight

The next morning, I woke with a massive ache in my head, and a moderate hematoma on my chin. I popped three Advils and washed them down with two cups of black coffee. Gabe's note was still haunting me from the edge of the table.

I was trying to make sense out of the information I had. It looked to me like the Saudis had dumped the bodies from the Mercedes GLS 600 they had leased from Fog City Motors, but why would they want one of the crowns now? They could have taken it before they dumped the body. And why does Ari Levine, who spies for Iran, want both crowns? I poured myself a third cup of coffee, then shook my head. I had forgotten about Katz. The Israelis also want the crowns.

And then, the sixty-four-dollar question hit me. If the Saudis don't have them, the Iranians don't have them, and the Israelis don't have them, then who in God's name does have them?

I needed to talk to Alex, but I didn't want to wait until the office opened. I checked my watch; it was six forty-five. I speed dialed her cell. It only rang once before she picked up. "Rick, what's wrong?"

"I'm not sure, but I need your help," I said.

"Anything. What can I do?"

"I need a political science expert. Any ideas?"

The phone went silent, and I assumed Alex was racking her brain. "Twenty years ago," she said. "I had a roommate in undergrad at U.C. Berkeley. When I went on to med school, she worked on a doctorate in poly sci. I'm not sure if she's still there, but I know she scored a great teaching position at Stanford. Her name is Amelia Harris. If you find her, say hello for me."

"Will do, Alex. I'll fill you in later."

I didn't feel much like eating with a sore jaw, but I managed to get a couple of scrambled eggs down without having to chew them. I showered and shaved and, by the time I was dressed, it was after nine. I Googled the number for Stanford University and called their HR department. "I'm looking for a professor named Amelia Harris. Is she still on your teaching staff?".

A very officious woman responded in a very officious manner. "I'm not allowed to give out that information."

"Why not?" I asked. "Isn't that public record?"

"Perhaps. I don't know."

"Well, do you have a brochure you give to future students that lists your professors?"

"Yes, we have that."

"So, it's no secret who your professors are?"

"No, it's not."

"Okay, let me ask again. Does Stanford have a political science professor named Amelia Harris?"

There was a pause. "Yes, we do."

"Well, now, that wasn't so hard, was it? Could I have her phone extension, please?"

"I'm not allowed to give out phone extensions."

"If I were her father and I had a medical emergency, could you give me her extension?"

"Are you?"

"No, but ..."

"Sorry, I'm not allowed to give out phone extensions," she said. This conversation was making my headache worse. I hung up and took two more Advils.

My office was only a couple of blocks from the Amtrak station, so rather than reporting for work, I bought a roundtrip ticket to Palo Alto, where Stanford University was located. The time schedule listed it as a twenty-eight-minute ride in each direction.

It always amazed me how thirty miles from San Francisco the fog would disappear, and the temperature would rise twenty degrees. It was a pleasant seventy-two and sunny when I stepped off the train. A young student, who I sat next to on the trip, steered me in the right direction and I walked the four blocks to the university's administration building.

A cute young lady, who struck me as a coed version of Taylor Swift, greeted me with a big smile. "Good morning, sir, may I help you?" She was obviously not the woman I had talked to on the phone.

I gave her my card and told her I was hoping to have a visit with Professor Amelia Harris. She looked at the card and her eyes opened wide. "You must be important," she said.

"Why is that?" I asked

"You have an 'ist'."

"An 'ist'?"

"You know, like neurologist ...entomologist ...psychiatrist ... what exactly is an odontologist?"

I didn't want to say it was a dentist who looked into the mouths of dead people, so I just said, "It's too complicated to explain."

"Wow, just like I thought." She scribbled on a piece of paper and handed it to me. "Professor Harris' office is in this building. Third one on the left."

Amelia Harris' door was locked, but a schedule of office hours was posted for her students. Today, they began at noon. I looked at my watch. A ten-minute wait was no big deal. I'd waited longer for a bowl of soup.

A few minutes after twelve, an attractive woman with short black hair, blue eyes and horn-rimmed glasses came walking down the hall. The first thought that jumped into my head was the number of guys who must have been hanging around Alexandra Keller and Amelia Harris' dorm room twenty years ago. She smiled and said, "You're either an old student or a young professor."

"Neither, I'm afraid." I handed her my card.

She read the title in a single glance and unlocked her door. "Come in, Dr. Rose, and tell me why I have the pleasure of your visit."

"I'm working for an old friend of yours, Dr. Alexandra Keller."

"Oh, how is Alex? We lost touch a few years back,"

"She's great. She says hello."

"So, you must be the specialist Alex counts on to identify the dearly departed through the use of your dental skills."

I was totally blown away. Amelia Harris, without having to consult with Google, described my position much better than I ever could. "That's me," I said. "But, Professor Harris, I'm here to request a political science lecture."

"I have twenty minutes before my first student arrives. Start by calling me Amy and tell me what you want to know."

"Okay, Amy, and, by the way, I go by Rick. Give me an overview of the relationships between Israel, Iran, and Saudi Arabia."

Amy rolled her eyes. "Rick, I spend two semesters every year trying to explain those relationships. Twenty minutes isn't going to do it."

"I get that. Just give me the Cliff Notes version."

"Okay, let's start with this. There's a lot of hatred in the Middle East. Israel hates Iran and Saudi Arabia ...Iran hates Saudi Arabia and Israel ...and Saudi Arabia hates Israel and Iran."

"I know that already, but why?"

Amy grinned. "And that, Rick, is what the two semesters are for."

I noticed that Amy's eyes lit up when she smiled. She reminded me of the other beautiful, intelligent woman I admired. No wonder they had been college roommates. I looked at my watch. "I still have fifteen minutes."

"Okay," she said. "Here we go. Since 1985, Iran and Israel have been engaged in an ongoing proxy conflict that has greatly affected the geopolitics of the Middle East, and has included direct military confrontations between Iranian and Israeli organizations—the Lebanon War in 2006, for example."

"Got it. They want to annihilate each other."

Amy nodded. "However, the Iran-Saudi relationship is a little different. Relations between Iran and Saudi Arabia have been strained over several geopolitical issues, such as aspirations for regional leadership, oil export policies, and relations with the United States, and other Western countries."

"So, how come the Israelis and Saudis hate each other?"

Amy walked to a wall that was covered by a world map and pointed to a tiny area nestled next to the Mediterranean. "For over a thousand years, this little piece of land was called Israel and for the next thousand it was called Palestine. Then in 1947, the United Nations partitioned it into two states: One for the Palestinian Arabs and one for the Jews. When Israel declared its independence in 1948, the official Saudi policy toward the conflict was support for the Palestinian Arabs against Israel ...and it remains the same to this day."

I was beginning to think two semesters wouldn't be enough for me. My head was spinning with a bunch of questions. "How do they keep track of one another?"

Amy threw up her hands. "The good old-fashioned way—they spy on each other."

My next question was to ask how they were able to wiretap each other in today's cyber-security environment, when I was preempted by a soft knock that came from the other side of door. Amy checked the time. "Free tutoring is over," she said. "Buy me dinner sometime, and I'll give you the next installment."

I stood and shook her hand. "Thanks Amy, I might just do that."

Thirty-nine

I got back to San Francisco a little after two and went directly to my office. When I stepped inside, Stella was typing up the latest report I had assigned to her. "Hey, Stella, give Dr. Keller a buzz and see if she's free."

"Will do," she said. "Oh, by the way, a guy named Moe called." She handed me a Post-it note. "He left this number."

I thanked her and headed for my private office, where I sat at my desk for a half an hour just staring at the number. "Should I, or shouldn't I?" I mumbled.

My indecision was interrupted when Stella buzzed in. "Dr. Keller is available for the next hour," she said.

Alex's secretary told me to go right in without knocking, which I reluctantly did. "Is this a good time?" I asked Alex.

"Perfect. Stella said you wanted to talk to me about something. I'm guessing maybe it has to do with your sudden interest in political science."

I took a seat facing her. "That's part of it, but I found out who that Jake guy is."

"The thug who threatened you?"

"Yeah, his name is Karim and he works for the Saudis."

"Saudi Arabia? They're involved in this?"

"Big time ...with emphasis on big. They leased the car that dumped both of the bodies."

Alex sat quietly while she processed this new revelation, then said, "So, they killed our John Does. But why would they want the crowns now if they already had first crack at them?"

"Crown," I said. "Singular. They only seem to want the crown taken from John Doe I and, if they killed him, it beats me why they wouldn't have taken it then. What I do know, they offered me three quarters of a million dollars for it."

Alex's eyes opened so wide I thought her lids would snap. "You're kidding me."

"Nope and that's two-fifty more than Ari Levine offered for the both of them."

"My God, what did you tell them?"

"That I'd think about it."

"But ...but, you don't have either of those crowns."

With a straight face, I said, "So, is that a problem?" I couldn't keep a blank expression for long and broke into a laugh. Alex had no choice other than to laugh along with me.

When we returned to sobriety, Alex said, "It looks like you're a popular guy in the Middle East. Israel, Iran and Saudi Arabia all want you as a friend."

"I don't think it's friendship they're after. That's why I needed a session with Amy. My knowledge of geopolitics doesn't go beyond the Mayflower leaving England for the new world."

"How is Amy?"

"Beautiful ...smart ...looks to be doing well. She says hello."

"Is she married?"

I thought back and couldn't recall if she was wearing a ring. "I don't think so. I didn't ask. Why?"

"You don't have a partner; maybe you should ask her out."

I was speechless. I wanted to tell Alex it was her, not Amy, that I wanted to spend time with, but there was no way I could say it, so I said nothing.

"Are you okay?" Alex asked.

"Fine ...I'm fine. She's not my ...my type."

I guess Alex sensed she had ventured into a sensitive space and changed the subject. "So, did you get the answers you were looking for?"

"Well, I understand why those three countries hate each other, and I understand they constantly spy on each other, but that doesn't help me figure out why a couple of gold crowns would be worth hundreds of thousands of dollars to any of them."

"Maybe it's time to bring Mike Kelly into the loop," Alex said.

I shook my head. "No, there's too many people already in this loop. A police captain won't help."

"Rick, with the threats, and the bribes, and the fact that you don't even have the crowns, you're in a vulnerable position. I'm worried for you."

I knew I was a guppy swimming in a school of sharks and, to be honest, I was worried for me too, but because I wanted to prove something to myself or more likely to Alex, I said, "I have a couple ideas." I was actually blowing smoke; I didn't have any ideas at all. "Give me a week and if I don't have anything more than I have now, you can turn the case over to Kelly or the CIA or both. We'll just send the bodies back to Israel and move on to our next unidentified corpse."

"Okay, a week. Promise?"

"Uh-huh, promise."

Forty

I went back to my office feeling dejected and worse, rejected. I was getting nowhere with the whereabouts of the crowns, and nowhere with a more personal relationship with Alex. I stared at the phone number Moe had given to Stella. I was curious why he was calling, and I was worried it might be to threaten my well-being.

There was no way of knowing how high Moe went in the Saudi chain of command. There was no doubt he was an enforcer; my jaw was proof of that, but his call surprised me. It was out of character for a tough guy like him to reach out by phone. I hesitated until my mother's words came back to me once again—in for a penny, in for a pound. I dialed his number.

The last time Moe greeted me, it was with an expletive and a knuckle sandwich; however, when he answered this call, he sounded like a graduate of a Miss Manners' master class. "Hello, Dr. Rose," he said. "Thank you so much for returning my call."

"Is this the same Moe that greeted me in Pacific Heights?" I asked.

If I were a diabetic, the sweetness he then laid upon me would have put me into a coma. "I am really sorry how I treated you at our last meeting. I'd like to invite you to the mansion to dine with me and my associates," he said.

I glanced over at the mirror on the wall. I wanted to confirm that I didn't look like the world's biggest idiot. "I don't think so," I said. "You guys don't have the greatest track record with hospitality."

"I understand. The world news media paints us as villains. So, where then, would you feel more comfortable for a meeting?"

I knew, if I met with this guy, it would have to be in a super public place. If he killed me, I wanted plenty of witnesses around. I had read in the *Chronicle*, just this morning, that the new venue built for the Warriors had opened a few days ago. I figured this might give me a chance to see how much influence the Saudis really have in San Francisco. "There's a basketball game at Chase Center tonight," I said. "Leave me a ticket at will call, and I'll meet you in the arena."

I had a few hours to kill before the game so I decided to use them searching for Gabe. I knew he liked to hang out in North Beach at the City Lights bookstore. I started there.

The old beatnik hangout from the fifties and sixties, where Jack Kerouac and Allen Ginsberg used to smoke weed in the basement, had a new twenty-first century clientele—much older tourists looking for ghosts, and younger ones looking for picture books of the Golden Gate bridge. Some walked the aisles, and others sat at tables skimming through books they had pulled off the shelves.

I moved my head slowly to the right and began a three-hundred-and-sixty-degree scan of the room. When I reached the two-fifty mark, I zeroed in on a guy in the corner who was trying to conceal his face behind the covers of a world atlas. I walked over to the table. "Go away," he said.

I sat next to him. "Gabe, what's going on? What's with that note you left?"

"I told you. I'm nothing but trouble for you."

"What are you talking about? I just want to help you."

Gabe pushed away from the table, collected his meager belongings, and held up his hand. "Don't look for me anymore," he said. Then he trudged out the rear exit.

I headed for Chase Center. If the newspaper was right, the cheapest tickets in the nosebleed section were going for four-hundred bucks a pop. I doubted Moe would find any at this late hour, but I knew I could use the walk and arrived there fifteen minutes before game time. I stepped up to the will call booth. "Rick Rose," I said.

The clerk thumbed through a bundle of envelopes in the 'R' section. "Sorry, sir, I don't see anything," she said. Just like I thought, the son of a bitch had no clout. "Could it be under another name?" she asked.

I envisioned Moe back at the mansion joking with his buddies about standing me up, but just in case, I said, "Maybe ...Doctor Rose?"

The clerk plucked an envelope from the 'D' bundle. "Here it is." She handed me the ticket.

The building was huge. In addition to all the photos, artwork and vendors that lined the corridors, the main arena was filled with about twenty thousand spectators—all eating and drinking while watching the Warriors take pre-game layups.

I handed my ticket to one of the ushers. She looked at it and said, "Section 103, row 1, seat 1. Wow, center court, front row." This guy, Moe, was beginning to scare me.

I hardly recognized my host. When he had assaulted me at the mansion, his face had a five-day growth and he was dressed in jeans and a torn sweatshirt. Tonight, he was cleanly shaven and wore what looked like a pair of Tommy Bahama slacks and a Ralph Lauren polo. "Welcome," he said. He pointed to a plate on his lap. "Can I order you a steak sandwich?"

Although it looked delicious, and I was starving, I didn't want to feel indebted to this guy. "No, thanks, I just ate."

We made small talk during the first half of the game, and Moe cheered loudly when Steph Curry made a half-court three to tie the game at the end the period. After most of the crowd rushed out to refresh their thirteen-dollar beers and twelve-dollar hot dogs, Moe got down to business. "Why aren't you taking the money?"

"Who said I wasn't taking it?"

"Karim."

"Is he your boss or something?"

Moe let out a belly laugh. "Hardly. He's my go-fer. I make all the important calls at the mansion."

"Well, I didn't tell Karim I wouldn't take it."

"Then let's seal the deal for the crown right now?"

I realized in that second that I couldn't bluff this guy much longer. But I had to try. "Give me the deal again," I said.

"It's the same as Karim told you yesterday—one million dollars."

I could feel my saliva glands stop functioning and my mouth dry up. Karim had said seven-fifty was the number—not a million. That sneaky bastard was going to skim a quarter of million for himself. "How do you deliver the money?" I asked.

"The simple way. No bank accounts, no wire transfers, just hard green cash in a Coleman cooler."

As much as I would love to have seen the second half, I knew I had to get the hell outta there. "We've got a deal," I said. Moe smiled and offered me his hand. I reached to shake it and noticed he was wearing a ring on his pinky finger. "That's an interesting symbol on top of your ring," I said.

He held it up for me to get a better look. "Oh, this. Yes, this type of star is a common symbol in Saudi Arabia. It's even on our flag."

"Interesting." I shook his hand and said, "I'll call you tomorrow."

Forty-one

I had a restless sleep that night and woke up at five a.m. drenched in sweat. I'd been in the middle of another one of my crazy dreams. This time, Moe was chasing me with a Coleman cooler, and when he caught me and opened the lid, instead of money, it was full of body parts.

I wasn't sure which was most disconcerting: the dream, the thought that I was supposed to deliver the crown to Moe today or the fact that I only had six days left before I admitted defeat to Alex. I took a cold shower and didn't bother to shave or comb my hair.

I never drink before breakfast; however, today I poured myself a double Virgin Mary. I was too depressed to go through the motions of making toast and coffee, so on the way into the office, I stopped at Big Louie's and picked up two large vanilla bean lattes with extra whipped cream.

Stella was her usual bubbly self. "Rick, you look like you had a bad night. Are you dating?"

"No, I'm not cheating on you, Stella."

She waved her hand at me. "Oh, you're such a kidder. Hey, are those lattes?"

They were still hot, so I gently placed them down and took a seat next to Stella's desk. I didn't think caffeine would help my morning sickness, but I was totally wrong. It jolted me out of my funk. "Messages?" I asked.

"Your new friend Moe ...said he's waiting for your call."

I banged my fist on the table. "Shit," I said.

"Rick, what's wrong?"

"Nothing ...no, nothing. This guy wants to sell me insurance. That's all."

Stella put her hand over mine and said, "Rick, I can tell you're in a bad place. You need some good company. I want you to join Chris and me for lunch today."

I don't know why I had planted that lunch idea with Stella, but I needed to backtrack it. I shook my head. "The last thing you and your boyfriend need right now is a chaperone."

"I want you to meet him. Please ...pretty please ...for me?"

Stella had me boxed into a corner, and I didn't want to disappoint her. "Okay, but I can't stay for long. What time and where?"

"Delancy Street Restaurant at twelve-thirty. I'll surprise Chris."

"I bet that'll go over real big. Okay, see you at twelve-thirty."

Most of my morning was spent in deep thought about the even deeper hole I had dug for myself. Ari was waiting to wire a half million dollars to an account for me in Monaco and Moe was waiting to stuff a million into a cooler for me—a quarter of which, by the way, Karim was planning to steal. I glanced at the time. Damn it. I was late for lunch.

The Delancy Street Restaurant wasn't really on Delancy street. It was on the Embarcadero—a boulevard that runs along the waterfront. It was less than ten blocks from my office, so I decided walking it would allow me to arrive fashionably late. I entered from the side door into the bar, which saved me the effort of going around the corner to the main entrance. I'd never been in this restaurant, but if the food was as inviting as the bar, having lunch with two lovebirds might not be as bad as I'd envisioned. I peeked into the dining room and spotted Stella and Chris in the corner. I was poised to step inside, when Chris turned his head and froze me in my tracks. Stella's boyfriend wasn't named Chris. His name was Karim.

I quickly did an about face, snuck out the side door and hoofed it back to the office. I was distraught. How could I tell Stella her boyfriend wasn't interested in her; he was interested in me.

Stella got back around one-thirty and banged on my door. "Who is it?" I asked.

"Goddammit, Rick."

I opened the door and Stella came storming in. "Why did you stand us up?"

"I'm sorry ...really. I had to take a call from Israel. Was Chris upset?"

"No, I never told him you were coming. It was going to be a surprise."

"I'll make it up to you ...promise." I gave her a little hug. "Forgive me?"

Her frown morphed into a smile. "Okay, you owe me, though." She left and closed the door behind her.

I spent most of the afternoon in a tug of war with my conscience. Down deep I knew I should come right out and tell Stella her new love was not only an imposter, but probably a killer and definitely a thief who was using her to keep tabs on me. He was undoubtingly fishing for information, which she was unwittingly providing.

On the other hand, in the interest of getting to the bottom of this clandestine mess, it might be useful to feed false information to Stella, knowing Karim would glean it from her. I knew, whichever way I chose, this wasn't going to end well for Stella.

The sounds of Stella's cheery voice and warm laughter radiating from the reception room made me feel like a total asshole. I tried to block them out, but that only switched my thoughts to remorse. How did I get into this mess, and what made me think I could navigate the world of espionage into which I had so arrogantly stepped?

It was obvious I couldn't control this situation by myself. I needed an ally in addition to Alex. I knew it wasn't going to be Ari Levine or Moe the Great, so I looked up the private cell number Dovid Katz had given me. I checked my computer for time difference; it was almost two a.m. in Tel Aviv. I didn't care. I figured spies expected calls in the middle of the night. He answered right away. "Katz."

"Dovid, this is Rick Rose ...in San Francisco."

"Who?"

"Rick Rose, from the medical examiner's office. I hope I didn't wake you."

I thought I heard a toilet flush, and then Katz said, "No, I'm in the kitchen. Why the call?"

"I need you here in San Francisco."

"Why?"

"Do you still want those crowns?"

There was silence on the other end of the line. I knew Katz was weighing his options. "Of course, I want them, but I'm not going to pay you for them."

"That was a misunderstanding. I don't need your money; I need your help. Trust me, it'll be worth your while."

"Okay, how's next week?" he asked.

"How's tomorrow," I said.

"I don't think I can do tomorrow. How's ..."

"Dovid, if you want those crowns, you'll be here tomorrow."

Again, there was silence on the other end of the line. I wasn't sure if Katz was fuming or figuring. After what seemed like forever, but was in fact only two or three minutes, he said, "I can catch a flight in about two hours. Have someone pick me up tomorrow morning at the El Al terminal ...ten-forty your time." He hung up.

Forty-two

I got to the El Al passenger gate a half hour before Katz's plane was scheduled to arrive. While I sat, I ran the details over in my mind. I knew who killed and dumped the John Does. I knew their deaths had something to do with the complicated Israel-Iran-Saudi relationships, and I knew all three countries wanted those crowns. But why did they want them? And where were they?

There had to be a common denominator. What is it ...or ...who is it? And then the proverbial light bulb went off in my head—Jim ...Jim Allen. He had investigated both crime scenes, while the bodies were still there. Jim had access to the autopsy records. Jim knew who wanted those crowns. And the biggest indictment of all; Jim was a bad cop.

The arrival of El Al flight 261 from Tel Aviv was announced over the public address system and fifteen minutes later, Dovid Katz and his sidekick Agent Levy exited the jetway into the lobby.

I greeted Dovid Katz and realized I'd never been given Levy's first name. "What should I call you?" I asked.

He laughed. "My name is Yechezqel, but I go by Zeke."

"Zeke it is then," I said. "I'll drop you guys at the Marriott, and we'll get down to work right after lunch."

~ * ~

I tried to keep Alex in the loop, but that didn't include my unproven suspicions about Detective Jim Allen. It also excluded my discovery about Stella's internet heartthrob. I wanted to spare Stella as much pain and embarrassment as possible.

Alex joined me in the conference room a few minutes before Dovid Katz and Zeke Levy arrived. "Okay, why are they here?" she asked.

"I invited Katz. He brought Levy with him."

"All the way from Israel?"

"Yeah, called him last night."

"So, what's the plan?"

"We need them and they need us. Maybe if we work together, they can go home with the crowns and take the John Does with them."

"But we don't have the crowns."

"Yet," I said. "We don't have them yet."

Stella announced the arrival of the Mossad agents who joined us at the conference table. She set down a carafe of coffee and a plate of chocolate chip cookies, then quietly slipped out of the room. "Well, they're not babkas, but they're pretty good," I said. Dovid and Zeke smiled and picked a couple from the plate.

"So, you said if I came here today, you'd give me the crowns," Katz said.

I shook my head. "No. What I said was, 'if you want those crowns, you'll be here today.'"

Katz looked confused. "So, do I get them or not?"

"We don't have them, Dovid, we never did."

Fire shot from Katz's eyes. "Are you shitting me? You called me in the middle of the night and dragged me seventy-five hundred miles to tell me you don't have the crowns?"

I raised my hands to hold back the onslaught. "Easy, easy. With your help, we'll find them."

Dovid stared at Alex. "Are you a part of this hoax?"

Before Alex could respond, Zeke stood up. "Dovid, relax and hear Rick out." I realized then why Dovid always brought Zeke along with him; he was Katz's calming influence.

Katz took a deep breath and leaned back in his chair. "Sorry," he said. "Okay, Rick, let's hear it."

"We have your comrades' bodies, but before they got to us, someone extracted those two crowns you're after. You have to tell us why they're so valuable, then maybe we can figure out how to get them back."

"I can't do that," Katz said.

Alex finally joined in. "You have to. You have no choice if you want us to be able to find them."

Katz looked over at Levy and then at Alex, "Could Zeke and I have a couple minutes in private?"

"Absolutely," she said. Alex and I stood and left the room, but before I closed the door, I could see Dovid and Zeke had already begun arguing.

I thought this was going to be a slam dunk, and we'd be back at the negotiation table in five minutes, but I was wrong. Five minutes passed, then ten, then twenty. "Did I miscalculate?" I asked Alex.

Alex had that rare ability to put people around her at ease. "Relax, Rick. You're doing fine."

"I wish I had your confidence."

She patted the top of my head like I had just survived my first day of kindergarten. "Patience, Rick, patience."

I checked my watch. Forty-five minutes had passed without the conference door being opened. My gut tightened, and the bitter taste of morning coffee rose in my throat. I'd grown up in a religious household, but I'd always questioned the existence of a supreme being. At this moment in time, I decided to hedge my bets and mumbled under my breath, "Please, God, don't make me look like a shmuck—not now."

Just two minutes short of an hour the door opened, and Zeke stuck his head out. "We're ready," he said.

When we returned, I noticed Katz had taken my seat at the head of the table; I took that as a metaphoric move to signal he was in charge. "Sorry about the wait," he said. "I called our Mossad director, and he called the prime minister, Chiam Weiss. Weiss, himself, signed off on this. Where would you like me to start?"

"Who, exactly, were the John Does?" I asked.

"Their names were Noam Sharon and Yael Ibrahim. You were correct, they worked for our Department 18 division."

"So, they were spies," Alex said.

Katz nodded. "Yes, they were our spies. Three weeks ago, we intercepted a communique that told us the Saudis were going to plan an operation that would give them a power advantage in the Middle East. It also told us the planning session was to take place at their mansion in San Francisco. We sent our guys there to discover what the Saudis were up to."

I had seen with my own eyes that the mansion was surrounded by a squad of armed men. "How did Sharon and Ibrahim breech their security?" I asked.

"There was a weeklong reception planned for dignitaries from the United States, and other friendly countries, to meet the representatives of Saudi Arabia. It was basically a seven-day propaganda PR party. Which one of our guys was dressed in a tux?" Katz asked.

"Our first John Doe," Alex said.

"That was Noam Sharon. He attended the reception, with forged documents, as a member of the British delegation."

"So, I assume the guy in the tee shirt and coveralls was Yael Ibrahim," I said.

Zeke took a photo from his wallet and slid it across the table to me. It showed two guys with arms over each other's shoulders. "Yael and I had been friends ever since we entered the Mossad as rookies. He was a gentle guy ...but fearless. He got into the mansion as part of a repair crew that was working on the antiquated plumbing."

Both Alex and I were mesmerized. This was real spy stuff. Stuff you'd find in a Tom Clancy novel. If Katz had said one of his spies was named Jack Ryan, I would have believed him. "Where does a spy look for secrets?" I asked.

"Computers," Katz said. "Noam was one of the best hackers in the world. He could get through passwords and firewalls faster than I could hit the enter key. Yael was just there as a backup to Noam. Once Noam had the secrets, he was to give a copy to Yael just in case Noam couldn't get them out of there on his own."

"How?" I asked.

"How, what?" Katz said.

"How were they supposed to get the information out?"

For the first time since the chocolate chip cookies were delivered, Dovid Katz and Zeke Levy smiled. "Inside the crowns," Zeke said.

Forty-three

Our meeting with Katz and Levy continued until almost four o'clock. After sending them back to their hotel, I stopped at Stella's desk and asked the usual question. "Any messages?"

She handed me a note. "Same old, same old: your Amway dealer, Joselle Freeman Rosenkofsky, your insurance salesman, Moe with no last name, and your lunch and dinner partner, Ari Levine."

I had no intention of talking to any of those people today, so I stuffed the note into my pocket. "Big date tonight?" I asked.

"Yeah, really exciting. Chris is taking me to Pier 39 for dinner."

"Sounds great. Hey, would you have time to type up a memo I can send out first thing in the morning?"

"Sure, what do you want it to say?"

"That I've located the crowns, and we'll be turning them over to the Israelis before they return home tomorrow afternoon."

"That's it?"

"That's it. I'll decide tomorrow who gets copies." I waved goodbye and took a taxi to my apartment.

~ * ~

I'm one of those guys who needs at least seven hours of sleep to function the next day, so ten o'clock was my usual bedtime. That night, I didn't even bother to take off my shoes; I knew I'd be going out around eleven.

I was off by fifteen minutes. At ten-forty-five I answered my cell phone. "Is that you, Karim?"

There was a pause, where my caller was obviously trying to figure out how I knew it was him. He wasn't able to put two and two together and said, "We have to talk."

"Okay, talk."

"Not over the phone. Meet me in front of Scoma's on Fisherman's Wharf—eleven-fifteen."

"I'm in bed, Karim. Call me in the morning."

"No, goddammit, Rose, if you don't show up, I'll blow your brains out. I mean it this time."

"Well, since you asked me so nicely, I'll be there." I hung up.

I wanted Karim to be agitated, even more than he already was, so I purposely arrived an hour late. Fisherman's Wharf, one of San Francisco's main tourist attractions, had no shortage of great restaurants. I always loved the smells that seeped into the air around them: fresh fish, melted butter and sauteed garlic. I paused for a moment, inhaled the aroma, and then continued on.

Karim saw me meandering toward him and came running with sweat dripping from his sideburns and running down his cheeks. "Where the fuck were you?" he asked.

I looked at my watch. "It's twelve-fifteen. I'm right on time," I said.

"Eleven-fifteen ...I clearly said eleven-fifteen, you asshole. Now listen to me ..."

I'd left my line in the water long enough. Now was the time to reel it in. "No," I said. "You listen to me. You want something I have and unless you apologize for being such a prick, you're not going to get it."

By then, Karim was totally drenched in perspiration. "Okay, I'm s ...sorry."

"That's better. Now, what do you want?"

"You promised Moe you would sell us the crown for seven-hundred and fifty-thousand. Now I learn you're doing business with the Israelis."

It was time for the gut punch and I have to admit, as evil at it may sound, I took great pleasure in delivering it. "You have it wrong," I said. "I promised to sell it to Moe for a million, not seven-fifty. It looks like the courier is planning to keep a quarter of a million for himself." Karim's jaw dropped. He was speechless. "What do you have to say about that ...Karim? Or should I call you Chris?"

"I ...I can explain," he said.

"No, you can't. Look, my boss, Dr. Keller, knows all about this and wants me to throw you to the wolves, but I like you, Karim ...and so does Stella. So, I'm going to make you a deal. You tell me about the crowns and the dead bodies, and I'll give you a twelve-hour head start before I tell Moe you were planning to steal Saudi money."

The blood drained from Karim's face and his usual dark complexion turned to a light shade of gray. "No, please ...please don't do that."

I looked at my watch again. "You're using up time. Less than twelve hours now."

"Okay, okay. What do you want to know?"

"You found those two guys were spying on you in the mansion. Is that right?"

"Yeah ... yeah, that's right."

"You killed both of them. Correct?"

"Someone else did. I just dumped the bodies."

"You mean Moe killed them."

I thought Karim was going to throw up right in front of me. "I ...I can't say," he answered.

"I'll take that as a yes. So why didn't you dump both bodies at the same time?"

"We didn't know there were two spies until later. It wasn't until after we got rid of the first one that we realized there was second spy. We beat the shit out of him until he told us about the gold crowns."

"So, you yanked the crown out of his mouth."

"Yeah, and that's when we figured the first guy must have had a gold crown in his mouth too, but by then it was too late. He was already in your morgue."

"So, what secrets were hidden inside those crowns?"

"I don't know. I just do what I'm told and don't ask questions. Please, Dr. Rose, give me more than twelve hours."

"I'll give you twenty-four, but I want something else from you."

"Anything ...anything."

"You leave a text message on Stella's phone tonight. You tell her you're married and decided to go back home to your wife. You tell her you're sorry, and she'll never hear from you again."

"Yes, yes, I'll do it."

I pointed toward the parking lot. Karim took off running.

Forty-four

The next morning, I got to the office around eight-thirty and wasn't surprised to see a temp sitting at Stella's desk. "I'm Dr. Rose, are you filling in today?" I asked.

"Yes, Doctor, I'm Jackie, Stella called in sick. I see she typed up a memo yesterday. Do you want me to send it out?"

I shook my head. "No, you can tear it up." I gave Jackie Katz's room number at the Marriott and asked her to call him and set up a meeting in our conference room at ten o'clock. Then I stepped into my office and called Ari Levine. He picked up on the first ring. "Rick, I've been trying to reach you for a couple days," he said.

It was tap-dancing time again. "Sorry, I had a couple new corpses to meet."

"I understand, you're a very busy man. I've contacted my friends in Monaco, and they're ready to go. Are your partners up for the deal?"

I couldn't tell Ari the Saudis had one of the crowns and the other was still missing, so, as usual, I had to lie like a rug. "Yeah, they're good with the deal, but they don't like the idea of running the money through a casino."

"No problem. Do you want it put in an offshore bank account or in bitcoins or cash? Whatever. Just name it."

"How about gold?"

"Sure, we can do that, but it will take a few days to get hold of it."

"We can wait. Call me when you have it."

I hung up the phone and thought about Stella. I was heartbroken for her. I wished I could have let her down slowly, but that would only have prolonged her agony. From personal experience, I knew the knife of betrayal digs deeply, but the wound would eventually heal. A series of little cuts would bleed forever.

My brain shifted gears, and I went back to thinking about who might have the missing crown. Yesterday, I figured it was Jim, but maybe it was someone else. As much as I hated to even think it, Helmut, my lonely pathologist with the classical music, had exclusive access to John Doe I for forty-eight hours before I had done his oral exam—maybe, just maybe.

I wanted both Jim and Helmut at the meeting when Dovid Katz and Zeke Levy told us anything more they were willing to tell us. I called Jim on his cell and Helmut in the morgue to make sure they would join us at ten.

I stepped into the conference room five minutes early and set my notes, readers and a cup of coffee at the head of the table; I wanted Katz to know who was back in charge. When he took his seat at the table, he gave me a subtle nod. I nodded back.

I went right to the point. "I learned last night that we're only searching for one crown, not two." I looked at Levy. "Zeke, I'm sorry to be the one to tell you, but your friend Yael Ibrahim was beaten until he gave up the information about the crowns. They ripped it out of his mouth before they killed him."

Zeke tilted his head toward the ceiling, but his expression didn't change, and he didn't speak. Dovid reached over and gave him a pat on the back. "How did you find out?" Zeke asked.

"If I told you, it would cause someone who doesn't deserve it a lot of discomfort, so I can't tell you. Let's just focus on the crown that's still missing from the mouth of your hacker, Noam Sharon. Dovid, you told Alex and me that your men were able to hide secrets inside those crowns. How was that possible?" Katz looked suspiciously toward the end of the table where Jim and Helmut were seated. "It's okay, they're part of our team," I said.

Katz nodded again. "Well, you already know we replaced Noam and Yael's lower left second molars with implants. By doing so, the gold crowns that fit over them could be made oversized and hollowed out to allow enough space to hide a micro memory card. The cards slipped into those compartments."

I tried to visualize the internal anatomy of an implant crown. "So, the crowns must not have been cemented in place."

"No, not when our guys entered the mansion," Katz said. "But, after Noam hacked the information from the Saudi computer and transferred it onto memory cards, he and Yael were to slip the cards into the crowns, and use a tube of dental cement to anchor them onto their implants."

Alex had an incredulous look. "I've seen micro memory cards. They wouldn't fit inside an area that small."

Dovid smiled for the first time today. "An example of Israeli ingenuity, Dr. Keller. Our computer engineers took the Micro SD cards that were developed by the SanDisk Corporation, right here in the Bay Area, and reduced them down to a size of five by five by one millimeter. The cards still remained compatible with the

TransFlash format San Disk had developed earlier, so we revised the program to enable us to read them."

"Then, whoever has the crown taken from Noam Sharon's mouth has the secret that was hacked from the Saudi computer. Is that correct?" Alex asked.

"They have it," Katz said. "But they probably can't read it without our technology."

I looked in Jim and Helmut's direction as I asked the next question. "If the SD card contains espionage secrets, what happens to the person who's caught with it?"

Katz thought over the question for a minute or two. "That depends. If the U.S. finds him, I think it's twenty years in prison. If we find him, it's life. If Iran or the Saudis find him, he's a dead man."

I closed the meeting and told Jim and Helmut they were excused. Without speaking, they shuffled out of the room. When the door shut behind them, Alex turned toward Katz. "Dovid ...Rick and I have talked this over; theoretically, our job is finished here. You've ID'd our John Does, and their bodies will be sent back to Israel, but we did promise to help find that missing crown, so we'll keep working on it until the end of the week. After that, although I hate to do it, I'll have to turn it over to the CIA."

Katz and Levy nodded. "Okay, we've got three days then," Katz said.

Forty-five

When I returned to my office, the message Stella had given me yesterday was still pinned to my blotter. As much as I wanted to ignore it, my conscience wouldn't let me. It wasn't that I disliked Josie—she was a good person, but I wanted to move on from her. This hounding me to be a sperm donor for her child was driving me nuts. If I were to father a kid, I'd support him and be a part of his life, but I'm thirty-four years old, and I don't know if I'm capable of a commitment that huge. Well, I at least owed her the courtesy of talking about it. I left her a message to meet me for lunch at the In-N-Out Burger on Jefferson St.

I have to admit I had an ulterior motive to meet Josie there. This was the place where Gabe said he had been working when he got the Merrill Lynch offer. I arrived a half an hour early and asked to talk to the manager.

A guy tall enough to play center for the New York Knicks approached my table. He was dressed in all white except for a red apron and the red short-billed baseball cap all the In-N-Outers wear. "You wanted to speak to me, sir?"

I tilted my head. It was a long way up to the face under the cap. "Yes, I'm Rick. Do you have a minute?"

He thrust out his hand. "Hal ...sure, I have a few minutes." He plopped onto a chair that was not designed for his physique, but he managed to fake comfort. "What's up?"

"Hal, how long have you managed this place?

He kind of stared into space while he did the math. "Two years next month."

"Do you remember an employee named Gabe ..." I realized for the first time I didn't know Gabe's last name.

"Yeah, sure. I remember him. Gabe ...Gabe Chamberlain... good worker, but ..."

"But, what?"

"But I had to fire him."

"Fire him? Why?"

"He was stealing."

"Stealing. Stealing what... french fries?"

"No, he was short changing customers and pocketing the cash."

"So, he never told you about being hired by Merrill Lynch?"

The big guy smiled and then broke into a hysterical laugh. "Merrill Lynch? Gabe? Maybe by that greasy spoon down the street—Merle's Lunch—but not by Merrill Lynch."

"Do you still have his application, by any chance?"

"I do, but I can't show it to you. You know ...rules stuff."

I handed Hal one of my cards. I was pretty sure he'd never heard of a forensic odontologist, and I suspected just the length of the title would impress him. "It's okay. I'm government," I said.

I wasn't sure if it was the title that had the impact or the little gold star at the bottom of the card, but he jumped up and said, "I'll copy it for you ...sir."

Josie arrived a couple minutes later and took the seat Hal had vacated. "Oh, Rick, it's so good to see you," she said.

Somehow, I'd forgotten how attractive Josie was. She had beautiful blues eyes and stunning long black hair that was pulled back into a ponytail. She looked like she was working out every day and probably had a BMI of around 8. "Yeah, you look healthy," I said.

I offered to spring for lunch. I ordered a double cheeseburger with fries for myself and a small salad without dressing for Josie.

"Are you going to do it?" Josie asked.

"What? Donate?"

"Yes. Please, Rick, it would mean so much."

"Don't you have a boyfriend or something?"

"I want my child to come from good stock. You're good stock, Rick."

I wasn't sure what she meant by good stock. I was a mediocre dentist, a reformed alcoholic and an unproven forensic odontologist. In my own mind, I was a nothing burger who was trying anything and everything just to become relevant. "I'm not ready to become a father," I said.

"I won't tell anyone who the father is. No one will know."

"I would know ...and besides ...I can't be a father by way of a test tube."

Josie didn't respond and when Josie doesn't respond, I know her brain is in high gear and ready to downshift into overdrive. "How about the conventional way then?"

"You mean ...?"

"Like the old days. We have a few glasses of wine; we make out, and we end up in bed."

"I don't drink wine anymore."

"Oh, yeah, I forgot. Well, we'll skip the wine then."

"Josie, I don't think this is a good idea."

She reached across the table and put her hand over mine. "Rick, you look lonely. Are you lonely?"

"Not that lonely."

"What if you had company every night?"

Uh-oh. I was getting really uncomfortable with the direction this conversation was going. "No, Josie. We're not getting back together."

"I'm talking about Einstein."

"The cat? You'll give me the cat?"

"A trade. One night with me for a lifetime of nights with Einstein."

"You can't be serious."

"Very serious. Think about it."

I did, and it wasn't that bad an offer. I missed that little guy inching his way under the covers and rubbing his neck next to my shoulder while he purred himself to sleep. My thoughts were interrupted by Hal, who dropped an envelope on the table. "You didn't get this from me," he said, and walked away.

Josie pointed to the envelope. "What's that?"

I tucked it into my pocket. "Recipe for the animal fries. So, when?" I asked.

"I'll bring Einstein over tonight."

"And ...the other ...?"

"I already checked my ovulation calendar. Next Tuesday is the day."

"We'll have to talk about child support and visitation."

Josie smiled. I knew that smile. It was the one she always used when she knew she had me. "That's not a problem," she said.

I stood to leave. "Eight o'clock. Bring his litter box."

Forty-six

I left the office around five and decided to skip eating out. I was tired of being that guy in the restaurant who sits all alone, while the other tables are filled with laughing couples. When I was drinking, I used to anticipate five o'clock. It began happy hour. But tonight, all I had to look forward to was one of my make-believe cocktails and a frozen dinner. Damn, how I hated being a bachelor.

Ever since I had talked to the In-N-Out manager, something was eating at my brain, but I just couldn't get hold of what it was. Then on my way home, while sitting in the back of a cab, it hit me. It was that name—Gabriel Chamberlain. Somehow it had a familiar ring. I had either read the name in a newspaper or seen it on the internet.

As soon as I got into to my apartment, I fired up my laptop and Googled *Gabriel Chamberlain*. It went right to Wikipedia and the heading *Basil Chamberlain Financial Dynasty* popped up. It seems that the family accumulated almost five-hundred million dollars over the span of its first four generations, and the present fortune, now valued at over nine-hundred million, was under the control of two brothers: Richard and William Chamberlain. The third brother, Gabriel, had been disinherited in November of 2018.

I thought about what I had just read. What were the odds Gabe was the brother? There must be hundreds of Gabriel Chamberlains in this world. Why would I even think a homeless guy, who eats out of a dumpster, could be the disinherited heir to a nine-hundred million dollar fortune? I closed my computer and went to the refrigerator in search of something for dinner.

~ * ~

Josie was OCD when it came to appointments. She buzzed my apartment at exactly seven-fifty-nine. I was having second thoughts about the deal I had made with her. The part about Einstein appealed to me and doing the deed wouldn't be all that bad, but was I ready to be a father? I wasn't really sure.

I didn't respond to the first buzz or for that matter the second either. When Josie leaned on it for three long jolts, I acquiesced and pushed my speaker button. "Who is it?" I asked.

"Goddammit, Rick, you know who it is. Buzz me in." I unlocked the door and left it ajar; in about two minutes, Josie pushed it open and stormed in. Poor Einstein was peeking from his carrier with eyes wide open. "Are you reneging?" Josie asked.

I'd forgotten how cute that little guy was—all white fur with patches of black around each eye. I opened the cage, gently lifted him out and held him to my chest. "Hello, Einstein," I said. He purred and kneaded his claws into my shirt.

"Well, are you?" Josie said.

"Am I what?"

"Reneging?"

"No, did you bring any cat food?"

Josie took a dozen cans out of the litter box she had brought with her. "This will get you started." She turned and opened the door. "My house ...Tuesday ... nine o'clock. And wear that cologne I like." She slammed the door behind her.

Einstein and I were getting reacquainted when my phone buzzed. I was pretty sure who it was; I pushed the green circle and answered. "Is that you, Moe?"

"What the fuck is going on?" he asked.

"I don't know... what do you mean?"

The cordial and polite Moe had obviously disappeared and the a-hole Moe had returned. "Listen, smart ass, you may think you're brighter than me, but you're not. We had a deal and you're going to honor it or—"

"Who said I wasn't going to honor it?"

"The day before yesterday was when we were supposed to close the deal. That day is gone and so is the next. As a matter of fact, today's almost over. Now, are you starting to figure out why I might think you're double-crossing me?"

I looked at the wall clock. I told Karim I'd give him a twenty-four-hour head start, but only twenty had expired. What the hell, that was close enough for me. "Where is Karim?" I asked.

There was a long pause on the other end of the line before Moe spoke. "Why? What's he have to do with this?"

"He's a traitor," I said. "He was planning to steal two-hundred-and fifty thousand dollars of Saudi money before he delivered me my share."

"I don't believe you."

"Why don't you ask him? He's in the mansion, right?"

This pause was twice as long as the previous one. "Uh ...he hasn't been around today."

"Well, I've got news for you. He not going to be around at all anymore."

"Are you saying he's dead?"

"I'm saying he's dead to you. Check it out. In the meantime, I'm not doing business with you until you clear the snakes out of your pit, so call me back when you have it all figured out." I hung up.

Forty-seven

Early the next morning, when I arrived at the office, Stella greeted me with baggy lids and bloodshot eyes. I'd already decided, as guilty as I felt, that there was no upside in telling her she had been duped into giving up information or in telling her I was somehow involved in her misfortune. "Are you all right?" I asked.

She blew her nose into a cloth handkerchief and tucked it back under the sleeve of her blouse. "I'm okay."

I took her hand in mine. "Do you want to talk about it?"

"You have work to do."

"This is more important right now. Let's hear it."

Stella retrieved the hanky and dabbed the corner of her eye. "Chris texted me a 'Dear John' letter."

"So, the relationship is over?"

"The sonofabitch is married."

"Oh, that's awful," I said. "I'm so sorry, Stella."

"Don't be. I should have listened when you warned me to be careful of internet romances."

"I'm still sorry. How about we have lunch today?"

"Thanks, Rick, I'll be okay. Maybe we can do it after I get over this."

"That's fine. Whenever you're ready." I gave her hand an extra squeeze and headed for my office.

Before I closed the door, Stella raised a finger, "Oh, Rick, hang on a minute." She took a small package from her top drawer and handed it to me. "This was in front of the door when I came in this morning," she said.

I sat at my desk staring at the package. It was nothing more than a brown paper bag tied at the top with a piece of string. Across the front, written in pencil, were the words: *For Dr. Rose*.

I could tell my body was getting a shot of adrenaline by the way my hands began to tremble. I tried to steady them, but when that didn't work, I just tore the bag open with my teeth. A small Planters Peanuts can made a clanking sound as it dropped onto the desk.

I flipped off the plastic lid and resting inside the can, on top of a piece of wrinkled note paper, was a gold crown. I placed the crown on the desk and flattened out the note. All it said was: *I believe you've been looking for this.*

There was little doubt in my mind this was the crown taken from Noam Sharon, our John Doe number one, but to make sure, I turned it over and looked at its internal form. When I look inside an implant crown, I expect to see a lot of metal with a vertical tunnel that the implant-post fits into. This crown had very little metal and no tunnel. It was hollow, and I could see there was something wedged deep inside. I didn't try to dislodge it. After almost a month of busting my ass to find this thing, I wasn't about to screw it up now. I carefully placed the crown back inside the peanut can.

I had Katz's number in my contact list and tapped it twice to dial. I guess my number was on his list also. He picked up with, "Rick, why the early call?"

"Grab Zeke and get down here ASAP," I said. Katz didn't ask why, or for that matter say another word. I figured he was used to this type of thing and didn't want to waste time on pleasantries. He was probably knocking on Levy's door before I hung up.

I stepped into the reception room and Stella actually gave me a weak smile. "Feeling better?" I asked.

"Much," she said. "It's good to be back at work."

"That's great. Would you call Dr. Keller and tell her I need her in the conference room in a half an hour."

Stella jotted Alex's name on her blotter. "Anyone else?" she asked.

"Yeah, call the morgue and tell Dr. Reingold to be there and if you can find him, get Detective Allen there also."

As I sat by myself at the conference table, I reflected on my first month at this job. If the past was any indicator of the future, I'd need a lot more than $136,400 to keep me here. But the more I thought about it, the more I appreciated the perks that came with the position: three weeks of paid vacation, sick leave, medical insurance and a chance to see Alex Keller five days a week.

The sound of voices approaching woke me from my day dreams. Katz and Levy stepped into the room, and I stood to greet them. "The others will be here shortly," I said.

Within five minutes, Alex showed up with Helmut close behind. I looked at my watch and decided if Jim was really interested in being here, he would have been by now. "Let's get started," I said.

Normally, I'm not one who has a flair for the dramatic, but this morning I made an exception. I had borrowed Stella's spare handkerchief, and now I spread it out on the table with all its lace edges showing. In the middle of it, I placed the gold crown. The way everyone's mouth dropped open, one would have thought I was presenting the Hope Diamond. I gently slid it across the table to Katz.

Just as Dovid began to inspect it, the door opened, and Jim came barging in. "Sorry I'm late," he said, and took the spot next to Alex. She whispered something in his ear. He frowned and moved over one seat.

Katz reached into his pocket for a keychain that had a small magnifying glass attached. He put it under his right eye and focused on the inside of the crown. "This is it," he said. "Does anyone have something sharp?"

I handed him the pocketknife my dad had given me when I left Brooklyn to go to L.A. "To protect yourself from all those kooks in California," he'd said. A hint of a grin showed on my face—if he only knew.

Katz opened the smallest blade and slipped it inside the crown. He gave it a twist and out came the tiniest memory card I'd ever seen. It was no bigger than one of the peanuts I'd expect to find in that Planters can.

He took out his cellphone and began working the internet. When he had the information he needed, he gingerly folded the handkerchief over the memory card and handed it to Levy. "Use your credentials and get on the next El Al flight to Tel Aviv. It leaves in a little over an hour." Zeke put the treasure in his briefcase and rushed out the door.

I turned to Katz. "What now?" I asked.

"Our tech department is the only place in the world that can read this card. They'll send me an encrypted email when they find out what's on it." He looked at his watch. "Zeke should be there by midnight California time. I'll have the information by two a.m."

"Then, let's meet here at two," I said. I looked at Helmut. "You don't have to come." He dropped his head and shuffled out.

We all stood to leave and Katz turned to me. "Where did you find it?" he asked.

When I was in middle school, we read *The Devil and Daniel Webster*. I didn't get the ending then, but I get it now. Alex and I had made a deal with Jim to stay out of our way and in return we promised to give him all the kudos from this case. It was time to pay the devil. "Detective Allen found it," I said.

Katz shook Jim's hand. "That's great work, Detective." Jim smiled and peeked at Alex. She bit her lip and made a beeline to the door.

Forty-eight

My first case, which turned out to be more of a detective caper than a forensic puzzle, was rapidly approaching conclusion. However, there were a few loose ends—ends I wasn't sure I could tie into a bow without first creating a knot.

Alex and I were well aware that when Katz learned the secret contained on the memory card, he was under no obligation to share it with us. We hoped, in spite of our shaky start with him, he would confide in us at the upcoming meeting. Alex was confident, but I was worried, in spite of today's success, that we had burned our bridges with Katz when we left him scratching his head at the Ben Gurion airport.

I was also worried about the deep hole I had dug with both Ari and Moe. Each was convinced I was going to sell him the crown, and if I couldn't dig my way out of this mess, I was toast.

There was one other loose end, but it was personal. It was Gabe. He disappeared, leaving a myriad of unanswered questions: Who was he, really? Why was he running from me? Should I look for him, and what would I say if I found him?

This was one of those times when I wished I wasn't on the wagon. In the old days, I'd lean on a martini or a Jack-on-the-rocks to soothe my nerves. Now, it was a drink from a bottle that looked like beer and kind of tasted like beer, but wasn't really beer—sort of like those hamburgers that looked like meat, tasted like meat, but were made from tofu or some other crappy substitute.

I was rescued from philosophizing about alcohol by the familiar voice coming through the intercom. "Dr. Reingold is here. He'd like to speak with you," Stella said.

This was a first, the first time Helmut had visited me. All our other one-on-ones had taken place in his office—the morgue. "Send him in," I answered.

The minute he stepped through the door, I could see he was uncomfortable. His head had a little twitch, like a nervous tic, which I'd never seen. I rose from my chair and went to greet him. "Hey, buddy. What's up?" I shook his hand. It was cold and clammy.

"Rick, should I resign?"

"Resign? Why would you want to do that?"

"I know why you invited me to that meeting. You think I was the one who stole that crown."

"Did you?"

"No, I swear."

"Then, there's nothing to resign over."

Helmut didn't answer. He had a glazed look in his eyes and just stared off into the distance. I knew he was someplace else. "Helmut," I said, loudly enough to snap him out of his trance. "Then there's nothing to resign over."

He began to tear up, then began to sniffle, and then broke into a sob. "I ...I wanted you to like me. I even thought maybe I could be your friend ...but ...now you think I'm a criminal."

I put my arms around him like I would for a crying child. "It's okay," I said. "I don't think that at all."

"Then, why ...why did you tell me not to come to the meeting tonight?"

Helmut was partially right. For a while I did suspect him of stealing the crown, but he was wrong about why he wasn't invited to the meeting. When I told him not to come to tonight's meeting, I already knew he had nothing to do with the missing crown. I'm no psychiatrist, but I knew this guy was as genuine as they come.

"I'm so sorry, really sorry," I said. "It was unforgivable of me to think you may have had the crown ...and I do want to be your friend. Can we be friends again? Please?"

He pulled away. "I ...I'd like that."

I patted his back. "Just so you know why you aren't invited tonight—the meeting is going to have some real sensitive stuff. I'm not sure Katz will even share it with Alex and me."

"What about Jim?"

"He doesn't know it yet, but he won't be there either. Hey, are you hungry?"

Helmut nodded. "Kind of."

"Great, I'm buying lunch ...and we're not eating in the basement."

Helmut had never been to a kosher Jewish delicatessen, so I took him to the New York Deli, ironically located on Sacramento Street. I ordered a pastrami on rye with kosher dills, extra hot mustard and a helping of potato latkes smothered in sour cream. Helmut had turkey on white bread with sweet pickles, light mayonnaise and a bag of chips. So much for introducing him to ethnic food.

When I got back to the office, I had one call to make before tonight's meeting. I dialed it from my contacts list. "Jim, this is Rick."

"Hey, man, how you doin?"

"I'm doing fine. You?"

"Great. Ever since you gave me credit for finding that crown, I've been a local celeb down here in the precinct."

"Glad that's working out for you. Say, we postponed tonight's meeting. It's rescheduled for noon tomorrow."

"Okay, thanks for the heads up. See ya then."

Forty-nine

I was in my apartment watching *The Late Show*, just killing time, before my pick-up at one-thirty. The meeting was scheduled for two and I was only fifteen minutes away, so I'd be the first to arrive and get the office open. At around one-fifteen, my cell buzzed. The caller ID read: *D. Katz*. I tapped the green button and answered. "Dovid, is something wrong?"

"Not really. Are you still in contact with that man who calls himself Ari Levine?"

"Well, I have his cell number, if that's what you mean."

"I'm not sure if you know this, but he's an Iranian spy."

"Yeah, I know that."

"I need him at the meeting. Can you get him there?"

I scratched the top of my head. "I don't know. He wouldn't come to my office during the daytime; I doubt he'll want to come at two in the morning."

"Do your best. It's important."

Of all the numbers I had for Ari, the one with the 213-area code was the one he answered most often. I gave it a try. Surprisingly, he responded on the first ring. "Rick, I was hoping you'd call."

"At one-fifteen in the morning?"

He laughed. "I just hung up from my Swiss contact. The gold will be here tomorrow."

"Be at my office in forty-five minutes," I said.

"The gold hasn't arrived yet."

"Don't worry about the gold. Something important has come up. Just be there."

"I told you ...I don't like security cameras."

"Do you want the crowns?"

"Yes, you know I do."

"Then, be there in forty-five minutes. The security guy will let you in." I hung up.

I arrived at the conference room fifteen-minutes early and began pacing the floor. I was more nervous for this meeting than I had been for my own wedding. "Relax," a voice said.

I looked toward the door. "Oh, hi Alex. I hope tonight goes well."

She smiled. It was that same old warm smile she had showed three weeks ago when I first met her. God, it seemed like a year ago. "It will be what it will be," she said. "It's out of our control."

I knew she was right, but I hated not having control. I didn't have it when my parents chose my profession, I didn't have it over alcohol, I didn't have it over my marriage, and I didn't have it now. "Am I a wimp?" I asked.

Alex looked confused. "I'm not sure I know what you mean."

"You know—a guy who doesn't try because he's afraid he'll fail."

She laughed. "No, Rick, you're not a wimp. You weren't afraid to dig deep into this case, and you certainly didn't fail."

I wasn't sure about that. This case wasn't over yet and, with my luck, there was still time to mess it up. "I think someone's coming down the hall," I said.

Dovid Katz stepped into the conference room. For the first time, I grasped why this man was near the top of one of the most efficient intelligence organizations in the world. His shoulders weren't broad, but he carried himself like they were. He wasn't overly tall, but he stood so upright he appeared to be and when he spoke, everyone listened. This guy filled the room. "Is he coming?" Katz asked.

"Is who coming?" Alex said.

"Ari Levine," I answered. "Dovid asked me to get him here."

"So, is he coming?" Katz asked again.

"I dunno. I think so. I told him he's going to get the crowns."

"Good. Look, for security reasons, I had to destroy the printout from Israel," Katz said. "But you're both going to know what we found on that memory card. You understand this is classified and normally I wouldn't share it, but I need your help, so I'm willing to bend the rules."

"We understand," Alex said.

"Okay, first we wait for Ari Levine," Katz said.

We didn't have to wait long; Ari arrived five minutes later. When he saw I wasn't alone, he did an about face and retreated toward the door. I could feel my pulse throbbing through the arteries in my neck. I looked at Katz for help.

"Hold on," Katz said to Ari. "I'm with Mossad and tonight, you and I are going to make Israel and Iran partners for a while."

Ari spit on the floor. "And what makes you think we would want to partner with you?"

"To keep us from going to war with each other."

I could tell Levine wanted to get the hell out of there, but Katz's words were too compelling. He stepped back toward the conference table. "Let's hear it, and it better be good," he said.

Katz sat at the table, and we all followed his lead. He spoke directly to Ari. "Both our countries discovered the Saudis were planning something big, and you found out we had placed spies in the Saudi mansion. Is that right?"

It looked like Ari still wasn't sure if he wanted to be there, but he said, "For the sake of argument, let's say it is."

"It's my guess you somehow listened in on a Saudi communication and figured out they killed our guys for a secret hidden inside those gold crowns," Katz said.

Ari nodded. "That's correct, except the crowns disappeared." He pointed at me. "Our Dr. Rose here confiscated them."

"That's not entirely true," Katz said. "The Saudis recovered one of the crowns, but the other one disappeared. Actually, Dr. Rose never had it, but he pretended he did."

Ari looked at me with fire in his eyes. "You asshole," he said.

Anger rose inside me as I realized how illogical Ari's reasoning was. I was an asshole for lying about the crowns, but it was perfectly okay for him to tell me he was an Israeli spy when, in actuality, he was an Iranian one. I stood to confront him, and then my previous thought came back at me—there was still time for me to screw this up.

I sat back down and Katz continued speaking. "Well, the crown turned up yesterday, and I sent the memory card found inside it to Israel for decoding."

Ari began to fidget. "Get to the point or this meeting is over."

"The Saudis are planning an assassination attempt of Chiam Weiss, our prime minister, and they're going to make Iran the fall guy for it."

"Why should I believe you?"

Katz held up his palms. "What possible reason could I have for lying to you?"

Ari settled down. "So, they mean to blame us for the assassination?"

"Exactly, and if they get away with it, Israel and Iran will go to war, and we'll both weaken ourselves while the Saudis take over as the major power in the middle east."

Ari began to process this new revelation, while the rest of us sat in silence. "And even if they're unsuccessful, my country will be blamed for the attempt," he said.

Katz nodded. "That's right, they will."

Ari went back into thought mode. "So, we have to abort their mission before it begins. How do we go about that?"

Katz looked relieved. "We know where and when it's planned, and who's going to carry it out. Chiam Weiss is speaking next month at the United Nations meeting in New York City. A guy living in the San Francisco Saudi mansion, an assassin named Mohammad Jabbari, got the assignment. He goes by the nickname of Moe."

Until then, it felt like my blood pressure had remained relatively low, but Katz just sent it soaring through the roof. "Hold it, hold it. Did you say Moe?" I asked.

Katz nodded. "That's right, Moe. Why?"

"I know this guy; he offered me a million dollars for the crown. No wonder he wants that memory card before you guys get hold of it."

"Can you get us access to him?" Ari asked.

"Shouldn't be a problem. He's chomping at the bit to close the deal with me for the crown."

"Okay," Katz said. "Set up the meeting."

Fifty

When I returned to my apartment, I had a double Virgin Mary to calm my nerves, then I tapped in Moe's number. He answered with the cordial greeting, "Who the hell's this?"

"Rick Rose. Do you still want that crown?"

"I thought you were pissed off at me. Why the sudden change of mind?"

"For a million dollars I can change my mind," I said. "Do you want it or not?"

"I want it. When ...where?"

"Ten tonight ...the boathouse at Lake Merced."

Lake Merced is located in the southwest corner of the city, about a half hour away from the bustle of downtown. It's a place where Josie and I used to love spending a Sunday afternoon, renting a boat or just lounging on the nearby grass. During the day, it's overloaded with locals and tourists, but when the sun goes down it empties quickly. By nightfall, it's totally deserted.

As I thought about the plans I'd made with Dovid Katz and Ari Levine, my stomach began to tie itself in knots. I made a straight line to the bathroom. While I sat on the throne, I tried to figure out why I'd ever gotten involved in this operation. I wasn't a spy. I didn't work for some covert organization. I wasn't the political type; hell, I didn't even vote in the last election. I was just a journeyman dentist who graduated in the bottom of his class at UCLA. Well, not exactly the bottom. As I said before, I was ninety-first out of a hundred.

I knew it was too late for analysis and, like it or not, I was involved. I was involved up to my neck and, if I were really lucky, Mohammad Jabbari wouldn't kill me tonight.

I sat around for the rest of the day trying to figure out where I could find Gabe, but my jittery nerves wouldn't let me concentrate, and I fell asleep on the couch. When I woke up, Einstein was cuddling next to me, licking a spot of his fur he'd already licked a thousand times. When he began to purr, I figured it must be dinnertime.

I checked out my fridge. As usual, it was pretty empty. All I had was a frozen Salisbury steak, a box of pre-cooked chicken tenders and a bag of microwavable french fries. None of them looked very appetizing. I passed on dinner. Einstein, however, loved his meal. Josie always provided the best cat food money could buy. I served him the 'gourmet chunks of beef in succulent turkey gravy.' I have to admit, it looked a lot better than any of my stuff.

I played the script through my mind a couple more times while I kept peeking at the wall clock. Watching it didn't make it move any faster, but eventually it did strike nine. I kissed my little buddy goodbye, grabbed my jacket and headed out the door.

I had the cab drop me at the corner of Skyline Blvd. and Harding Drive. The boathouse was about a hundred yards away.

Tonight was only the second day of the new moon, and a cloud cover had settled in, making the sky totally dark. I cursed myself for not bringing a decent flashlight, but the one on my phone at least lit up the blacktop a few steps ahead. I followed the white line to the parking lot.

There were no cars in the lot. I kept walking toward a short set of stairs that led me to the deck of the boathouse. During the day, the view from this spot looked out over the water and to the golf course beyond, but the temperature had dropped to the dew point and fog was beginning to hover above the surface. The visibility was down to about ten or twelve feet.

My shoulders began to shiver and my knees uncontrollably tapped against each other. I have to admit I was scared, really scared. A voice came out of the abyss. "Rose, where are you?"

I turned my phone light back on and aimed it toward the sound. "Here, on the deck," I said.

As Moe emerged out of the darkness, with his face illuminated only by a flashlight, he looked like an apparition—almost ghostlike. "Why the fuck did you pick this place?" he asked.

I tried desperately to keep my voice from quivering. "Harder for your bodyguards to see me."

"There's nobody with me. I always work alone."

I didn't believe him, but it didn't really matter. "Where's the money?" I asked.

Moe smiled or should I say sneered. "Where's the crown?"

"It's not that I don't trust you, but just to be safe I hid it a few yards from here. What about the money?" I asked again.

"It's in a Coleman cooler, just like I promised, but I also stashed it on the way in. I don't trust you either."

I knew he was probably lying about the money, but frankly I couldn't care less. "Are you carrying a weapon?" I asked.

"Yeah, are you?"

I'd witnessed this scene in a dozen gangster movies, and I followed my memory. "No, pat me down if you like," I said. "Then throw yours out toward the lake."

Moe began at my shoulders and finished at my ankles. When he was convinced, I wasn't a threat, he tossed his pistol into the darkness. I suspected he had another one hidden somewhere. "What now?" he asked.

"I'll have the crown here in two minutes. You've got five to get the cooler. If you're not back by then, I'm out of here."

Moe took two stairs at a time from the deck and then raced toward the parking lot. As soon as he was out of sight, I followed the short footpath to the restrooms. I yelled into the men's. "He's on his way."

Dovid and Ari went sprinting by me on their way to the boathouse. I disappeared into the darkness and ran my ass off to get away from there.

Fifty-one

It was almost midnight by the time I saw the cab coming toward me on the boulevard. Rather than go back to my apartment, I asked the driver to drop me on the corner of Broadway and Columbus.

I had good reason to go to North Beach this late. The two most threatening things to the homeless are cold temperatures, and the fear of being a victim of a violent crime. Tonight, it was unseasonably chilly and with no shortage of criminals roaming the streets after midnight, most of the down-and-outers would be awake making their rounds.

We're all creatures of habit, and I counted on Gabe to be the same. I headed straight for the alley behind the Stinking Rose. Nothing had changed since the time I first met Gabe there almost a month ago. It was still poorly lit, still had a dumpster in the corner and still smelled from garlic.

My expectations were to find Gabe scavenging for food inside the dumpster or tucked away behind it fast asleep. I was disappointed on both counts. I looked at my phone. It was twelve-thirty—a little late for dinner and a little early for breakfast. I stuck with my intuition and decided to hang around.

The restaurant's food service had ended at eleven, but the bar stayed open until two. I sat next to a heavily made-up gal and ordered a Pellegrino on the rocks with a twist of lime.

"Buy me a drink, and I'll tell you what a single girl is doing here after midnight," she said. I was pretty sure I knew what she was doing, but I bought her the drink anyway. "Thanks, good lookin'. My name's Tootsie."

I shook her hand. "Rick."

She took a wad of gum from her mouth and wrapped it in a cocktail napkin. "You a tourist, Rick?"

Our drinks arrived, and I tapped my glass of sparkling water against her double scotch. "No, not a tourist," I said. "I live close by. Just looking for a friend of mine."

"Girlfriend?"

"No, a guy."

"You gay? You don't look gay."

"Really. How do gays look?"

Tootsie put her hand over her mouth. "Oh, sorry, man. I didn't mean to insult you."

I waved it off. "You didn't. I'm not gay."

"I've been making my rounds for a couple hours. What's your friend look like? Maybe I seen him."

I shook my head. "I don't think he'd be a client of yours. He's homeless."

Tootsie drained her glass and held it up for the bartender to see. "You'd be surprised. I do charity work all the time."

"Well, my friend's not your type."

"And what exactly is my type?"

I realized I had just committed the same profiling mistake she had. "Sorry," I said. "I'm an asshole."

Tootsie's second double arrived, and she drained half of it with one slug. "No, you're not. You seem like an okay guy. So, what's your friend look like?"

I gave her a full description of Gabe, right down to my pair of tassel loafers he was wearing when I last saw him. Tootsie pointed above her right eyebrow. "Does he have a fresh scar here?"

I almost choked on my sparkling water. "I can't believe it. Where did you see him?"

"I hang out at this scuzzy bar on Columbus, where drinks are only three bucks. The bartender lets homeless people use the bathrooms, and he slips a few bucks to them once in a while. "I remember your friend, 'cause he thanked the bartender and turned the money down. Said something like, other people needed it more than he did."

"What's the name of the bar?"

"Booze and Brews."

I signaled the bartender to refill Tootsie's glass, left two twenties on the bar, and kissed her on the forehead. "Thanks, Tootsie. Good luck tonight." I raced out the front door and headed up Columbus Avenue.

Booze and Brews was a little hole in the wall with a single-entry door and no windows. By now, it was going on two o'clock, and there were a lot of sad faces at the bar. The only people left were the ones who were desperate for a hookup.

The bartender put down a paper coaster and said, "Hey, bud, what'll it be?"

"I'm looking for a guy. He's homeless and has a scar over his right eye. Tootsie said you talked to him."

"You a cop?"
"No, I'm a friend of his."
"You look like a cop. Show me your ID."
I took out my business card and handed it to him. "I'm not a cop. I work for the city medical examiner."
"Is he in trouble?"
"No, I'm trying to help him out. That's all." I raised my right hand. "I swear."
The bartender pointed to a door with a placard that read: *Office*. "I told him he could lie down on the couch till closing time," he said.
I tapped on the door and entered before getting a response. Gabe looked up from the couch. "Rick, I told you not to look for me."
I pulled up a chair. "I had to. Tell me, Gabe, who are you? Really."
"I'm a pathological liar, Rick. That's who I am."
"So, everything you told me about yourself was a lie?"
"Not everything."
"What about growing up in a foster home?"
"Lie."
"French fry manager?"
"That's true."
"Working at Merrill Lynch?"
"Lie."
"Apartment on Jackson Street?"
"Another lie."
"Why? Why lie to me?"
"I told you, I'm a pathological liar. Sometimes I can't help myself."
"Maybe you're lying to me now," I said.
"Maybe ...but I'm not."

"Are you an heir to the Chamberlain fortune?"

Gabe ran his hand through his hair and gave out a sigh. "I was ... not anymore."

"What happened?"

"What happened? Greed happened."

"What d'ya mean, greed happened?"

"I wasn't happy being a millionaire, I wanted more. I wanted to be a billionaire ...so I tried to screw my brothers. I created a scandal and lied to the press and the courts. I swore under oath they altered the will and were trying to steal my share. They fought back and stripped me of everything. It turned out our father put a clause in the will. It disinherited anyone who contested it."

I felt like I was going to be sick. I wasn't sure if it came from being so totally deceived or because I knew this man I cared for had destroyed his life. "How did you get the crown from John Doe's body?" I asked.

"What makes you think I had the crown?"

"The back side of the note in the Planter's Peanut can had the silhouette of a wrench wrapped around a tooth. That's my mouth mechanic logo. You took a piece of notepaper from my apartment."

Gabe shook his head. "Pretty stupid of me, huh?" He dropped his gaze and stared at the floor. "I saw them dump the body in the alley and after they left, I searched it. The only thing of value was a gold crown in the back of the dead guy's mouth. I used a big pair of pliers I'd found in the junkyard to yank it out."

"Why didn't you sell it? The gold was worth at least five hundred bucks."

"Because ...I couldn't ...couldn't screw you like I tried with my brothers. You were the only person who ever took an interest in me." He began to sniffle. "I just couldn't ...couldn't ...I knew you needed it." He wiped his eyes with his shirtsleeve. "I want you to go now."

I stood to leave and reached for my wallet. "Can I loan you a few bucks?"

He didn't answer—just kept looking at the floor and shaking his head. I walked away and closed the door behind me. I never saw Gabe again.

Fifty-two

That had to have been one of the longest days in my life; right up there with the day I was caught treating patients with alcohol on my breath. By the time I got back into my apartment, it was after three a.m. and I was wiped out. I fell asleep on the couch and didn't wake up until noon. By the time I got to the office, it was almost two.

Stella looked up from her work. "Hi, Rick, rumor has it you did a real good job on the John Doe cases."

"Really, I didn't know anyone was watching."

Stella laughed. "Hello, there ... everyone was watching, and you're a local hero around here today."

I wasn't sure which rumor was circulating, but I figured last night's rendezvous must have turned out all right. "How are you doing?" I asked. "You seem in good spirits."

"Oh, I'm great. The more I thought about that jerk, the more I realized how lucky I was to be rid of him."

I gave her a thumbs up. "I'm happy for you. Hey, any messages?"

"Oh, I almost forgot. Dr Reingold wants you to meet him in the morgue. He's called three times."

I thanked Stella and took the stairs to the basement, where Helmut was engrossed in an operation on a new patient. I tapped him on the shoulder. "Hey, buddy, what's up?"

He pulled off his mask. "Hi Rick, I hear you're a celebrity."

"Hardly. Stella said you've been looking for me."

Helmut pointed to the corpse on the operating table. "A new John Doe for you to ID. Right up your alley—no identification and no prints in the databases."

I took one peek and didn't need anything more to ID him. The guy had two bullet holes in his forehead.

It appeared my standing in the forensic community had taken a giant leap forward, and I could think of no one I would rather celebrate with other than Dr. Alexandra Keller. I knocked on her door.

"Come on in, Rick," a voice from the other side said.

I stepped inside. "How did you know it was me?"

"I know your knock—gentle but commanding. Congratulations. Katz told me everything before he and Levine hightailed it out of the country."

"Did he tell you I was scared shitless and ran like hell to get out of there?"

Alex laughed. "No, I guess he left that part out."

Now was the time, I knew it. There would never be a better one. I took a deep breath and said, "Alex, how 'bout you and I go to dinner tonight and celebrate a successful case?"

I knew she would say yes. I could feel it in my bones. I knew it, until I didn't. "Oh, Rick," she said. "I just told Mike Kelly I'd go to dinner with him." She must have seen the disappointment in my eyes. "Say, why don't you come along. All three of us can celebrate."

I should have seen it coming. I knew Alex had fallen for this guy the moment he stepped into her office. He was like the prince holding the glass slipper. The last thing I needed was to be a third wheel in that relationship. "Maybe another time," I said.

Alex forced a smile. "Sure, some other time then."

~ * ~

So here I was, sitting alone in my apartment, on what should have been the best day of my life, longing to have dinner with a beautiful, intelligent woman. I looked at Einstein. "What d'ya think, buddy? Should I call her?" I know this sounds crazy, but I'd swear he understood. He jumped onto my lap and ran his sandpaper tongue over my cheek.

I looked at my phone; it was only four o'clock. I fumbled with my contacts list until I found the number and then hit dial. A familiar young voice picked up on the first ring. "Stanford University, how may I direct your call?"

I hesitated for a moment to build my courage, then blurted it out. "Professor Amelia Harris, please."

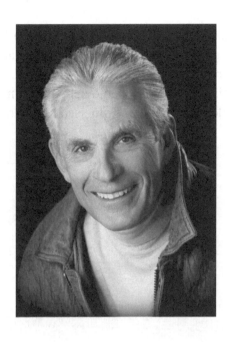

Meet Mike Paull

In 1998, Mike retired from the practice of dentistry in the San Francisco Bay Area and began honing his skills as a writer. Between 2010 and 2015, because of his love of flying, he self-published *Tales from the Sky Kitchen Café*, a book of aviation-based short stories and *Flight of Betrayal*, *Flight of Deception* and *Flight of no Return,* a three-volume mystery series.

In 2021, Mike was offered the opportunity to partner with Wings ePress, an independent U.S. publisher. Over the next three years, they released his new spy thriller series: *Missing*, *She's Missing* and *Missing in the Maldives*.

In the novel you just read, *The Mouth Mechanic*, Mike used his professional background to create the character of struggling dentist, Rick Rose. In so doing, he switched from his third person style of writing, used in previous novels, to the first person, in hopes of bringing his character more to life. He was successful; all the pre-publish reviews were glowing.

Mike and his wife Bev now enjoy spending time with family, two hundred miles north of San Francisco in Chico, CA.

Acknowledgments

I would like to thank my beta readers, the first to read and make suggestions to the manuscript: Barrie Scheid, an avid reader and a wonderful daughter, who doesn't shy away from criticizing her dad if it will make the story better. Brad Liebman, a great friend who keeps me writing even when I want to give up the ghost. Scott Paulo, who picks through my manuscripts with a fine-tooth comb and never seems to tire when I load him up with hundreds of pages at a time.

I also wish to thank my reviewers, who lent their time to read the pdf version of the book and write their opinions—excerpts of which are included in this final product: Author Lynn Solte. Author Andrea Barton. Author Karen Hudgins.

My thanks to the principals of Wings ePress Inc: CEO, Linda Voth and Executive Editor, Jeanne Smith who, through a labor of love, work around the clock on behalf of their authors to keep the engine of their independent publishing company running smoothly.

Last, but certainly not least, I thank my wife, Bev. After being conscripted to review every one of my ideas, sentences, paragraphs and rewrites, she still hasn't divorced me. Love ya, Bev.

Other Works from the Pen of Mike Paull

<u>Missing</u> - A bullet to the back detours a government agent's search for a hidden stash of gold.

<u>She's Missing</u> - When an intelligence agent's old partner goes missing, he puts his life on the line to find her.

<u>Missing in the Maldives</u> - While looking for the man who shot them six months ago, two U.S. intelligence officers search islands in the Indian Ocean only to get entangled in a web from which escape is difficult.

Dear reader,

I hope you've enjoyed reading this tale of forensic dental intrigue.
Your opinion is valuable to other
readers like you,
who may be looking for books like mine.

Please consider taking a few minutes to post a review, however brief,
on the site where you purchased this book
or on the Wings ePress web page.

You may also want to visit my author page
at the Wings' website, where you can find
all the other books in my series.

Thank you!

Mike Paull

Visit Our Website

For The Full Inventory
Of Quality Books:

<u>Wings ePress, Inc</u>

Quality trade paperbacks and downloads
in multiple formats,
in genres ranging from light romantic comedy to general
fiction and horror.
Wings has something for every reader's taste.
Visit the website, then bookmark it.
We add new titles each month!

Wings ePress, Inc.
3000 N. Rock Road
Newton, KS 67114

Made in United States
Troutdale, OR
09/27/2024

23168853R00139